Ambush at Amboseli

Ambush at Amboseli

Karen Rispin

Tyndale House Publishers, Inc.
Wheaton, Illinois

Scripture quotations are from the *International Children's Bible, New Century Version,* copyright © 1986, 1988 by Word Publishing, Dallas, Texas 75039. Used by permission.

Library of Congress Cataloging-in-Publication Data

Rispin, Karen, date
    Ambush at Amboseli / Karen Rispin.
        p.   cm. — (Anika Scott ; #4)
    Summary: When she and her family vacation in Kenya's Amboseli Game Park, twelve-year-old Anika Scott and her older half-brother Rick find themselves involved in chasing some elephant poachers.
    ISBN 0-8423-1295-1 :
    [1. Christian life—Fiction.   2. Elephants—Fiction.   3. Poaching—Fiction.
4. Brothers and sisters—Fiction   5. Kenya—Fiction.]   I. Title.   II. Series:
Rispin, Karen, date   Anika Scott ; #4.
PZ7.R494Am   1994
[Fic]—dc20   93-37801

Printed in the United States of America

00   99   98   97   96   95   94
8   7   6   5   4   3   2   1

Thanks to Marti Sheldrick for her help with information on elephants and poaching.

Chapter One

～～～～～～～～～～

Moonlight painted stripes on the mosquito net above my bed. It was the middle of the night. I lay still and listened to the sounds of the African night. I wanted to see if I could tell what woke me up. The lion roared again.

My heart beat faster. I grinned with excitement. We were in Tsavo National Park, and there were lions in the night. I put my hands behind my head and looked up at the thatched roof. My brother Rick was here.

For the whole twelve years since I'd been born, I'd never known I had a brother. Last month I found out. Actually, Rick was really my half brother.

Sandy was excited about having a big brother. I wasn't so sure. I mean, I had liked our family just fine the way it was before. Besides, Rick wasn't even a Christian.

I twisted uneasily against the sheets and remembered what had happened in the car yesterday. Mom had been quiet for a while. Suddenly she turned around toward us and said, "I'm so sorry." There were tear marks on her face.

My insides lurched. She kept talking. "Sin hurts for so long. Don't you girls ever make the same mistake I did. The Bible is right. Sin makes pain. It seems OK at the time but it makes pain." She paused, trying to get her voice in control. I stared at my feet.

"Mom, it's OK," Sandy said desperately.

"It's not OK!" Mom said. "The only hope we have for things to be OK is God's promise. In Romans 8:28, it says that God causes all things to work together for good for those who love him. I'm just holding on to that promise for all of us."

Daddy pulled the car off the road. Then he reached across to hold Mom's hand.

Mom said, "I know you're young for this, but I feel I have to tell you. I don't want you to repeat my mistake. I'm going to tell you what happened."

Sandy was staring at Mom, wide-eyed. I swallowed hard. I wanted desperately to know, but I hated this. Moms weren't *supposed* to have done things wrong.

Mom took a deep breath and started, "I was fifteen. Your grandfather had a hard time adjusting to having a teenage daughter. He spent a lot of time yelling at me. I felt like dirt at home. School wasn't much better. When Jim started asking me out, it made me feel better. He was one of the cute, popular guys and he noticed *me*. After a while he started asking me to have sex with him.

I was scared to say no. I felt like if I said no, then nobody would care about me."

She paused for a long time, looking down. Daddy rubbed her shoulder. Finally she said, "When Jim found out I was pregnant, he never talked to me again."

She started to cry. "I never saw the baby. I had to give him up. It was the only thing I could do."

Daddy hugged her. After a second I crawled into the front seat. Then Sandy came too. We all sat there in a hump hugging each other.

Daddy said, "Let's pray."

He thanked God that Rick had found us. Then he asked God to make things work out so it would be good for everybody. He prayed for Rick too, but that was nothing new. He and Mom have prayed for Rick ever since they got to be Christians. For a long time they didn't even know his name. They found out his name when Rick came to find us.

Rick came when we were climbing Mount Kenya. He didn't tell anybody he was coming. That was a very weird time for us! Sandy and I didn't even know about Rick before that. I was mad. I guess I was pretty rude, too. I didn't want anybody else in our family. God helped me get things straightened out. I even decided to pray for Rick.

We never got a chance to get to know Rick while we

were climbing Mount Kenya. Daddy decided he and Mom would take time off work so our family could go to the game parks, and Rick could go with us. Now we were here. Rick was sleeping in the cabin next to ours.

I stared up at the ceiling. It was so complicated. I still wasn't sure I wanted a twenty-two-year-old half brother. I turned over with a thump. My foot tangled in the mosquito net, and I shook it loose impatiently.

The lion started grunting. He sounded closer this time. Maybe it was a different lion.

"Huh! Huh! Huh!" The grunting built up to a roar that shook the air.

Sandy's bed squeaked and thumped. I looked over. She was sitting up. Her eyes were as big as saucers. Sandy is ten and she gets scared easier than I do. Her bangs were sticking straight up. That made her look even more scared.

"It's OK," I said. "The lions can't get in here."

"Shhh!" she whispered. "What if they hear you?"

The lion started to grunt again. We both held still to listen. It sounded as if he were right outside the thin wall of our cabin. Then he roared. The noise shook my insides and vibrated the bed. My muscles went stiff with excitement. A lion was right outside!

Sandy's bed was squeaking and thumping. Her sleeping bag looked like a worm with convulsions. She was crawling down to hide in the bottom of it. I stayed still, listening.

Finally the lion started to grunt again. He sounded farther away. He didn't roar. When he was quiet I said, "Sandy, you can come out. He's going away."

She didn't answer. I untucked my mosquito net and got out of bed. The concrete floor felt cool on my feet. I shook Sandy, "You can come out. You'll suffocate in there."

"Is he gone?" she asked in a muffled voice.

"Uh-huh," I said, and I jumped for my bed. We weren't supposed to go barefoot at Tsavo because of scorpions. Sandy sat up. Her hair was all over the place now.

I giggled. "Did you think that the lion wouldn't eat you in a sleeping bag sandwich if he wanted to?"

"He was close!" she said, wide-eyed. "I wonder if Rick was scared."

I grunted. I didn't feel like talking about Rick. Just thinking about him made my stomach hurt. I lay down with my back to Sandy. A nightjar called. The lion grunted again, farther off.

When I was almost asleep, I heard a door slam. Then there was a sound of running feet. I was too sleepy to wonder what was happening.

Our cabin had two rooms with a little porch in front. We ate breakfast at the table on the porch. Rick was supposed to come over from his cabin to eat breakfast with us. He hadn't come yet.

While we were eating, Dad said, "Do you know what Jesus told his disciples? In John 13:35, Jesus said, 'All people will know that you are my followers, if you love each other.'"

A brightly colored bird landed right beside my chair. It was one of the African starlings that always beg at these cabins. I threw it a bit of toast.

"Pay attention, Anika!" Mom said. "What your father is telling us is important."

I sighed and sat up straight. I could still see the bird out of the corner of my eye. It was eating the toast in quick pecks.

"Anika, what does the verse I just told you mean?" Daddy asked.

"Um, that we're supposed to love each other," I said, shrugging.

"It's more than that," Mom said. "How we get along makes a big difference to our witness."

"You mean Rick won't want to be a Christian if Anika and me fight?" Sandy asked.

Daddy laughed. "It's not quite that simple, but like the verse says, God's love should show in our actions to each other. That's what will draw Rick—God's love in action. If he doesn't see us loving each other, he will think the things we say about God's love are just a fancy lie."

"We have to love him too . . . right?" Sandy asked.

"Love and accept him," Mom agreed, and she added, "but the way we treat each other is just as important."

Strong in love and built on love, I thought, remembering the verses from when we were climbing Mount Kenya. I didn't say anything. I still wasn't sure I wanted to love Rick. I looked for the bird. He was behind Mom's chair. His head tipped as he looked on the floor for crumbs.

I slid out of my chair and held out a toast crumb on my hand. The bird hopped closer. Its bright red-and-blue front glowed in the sun. I held still with my hand out. Two more birds landed and hopped toward me. The first one was almost up to my hand now. His bright, beady eyes watched me. Suddenly all the birds flew away as Rick walked onto the porch.

I watched Mom hug him and Daddy shake his hand. Sandy was right in there too. Part of me wanted to walk over and be with everybody. But I couldn't. It was like my feet were stuck to the floor.

He's handsome, I thought. Rick was taller than Daddy. His eyes were the darkest blue. He had on shorts and a T-shirt. I could see big muscles in his arms and legs.

7

"Quit staring, Sis, and come say hi!" Rick said, turning to me with a grin.

I ducked my head and mumbled, "Hi!"

"So, did the lions steal your voice?" he asked.

"No," I said, and frowned at him. "Why? Did they scare you?"

"Yeah, did you hear them?" Sandy burst in eagerly. "They sounded like they were right outside!"

"Hear them!" he said. "I was halfway to the outhouse when the lion roared the first time. I dodged inside and slammed the door. Something ran across my foot, and I nearly died. It was one of those little gecko lizards that live on the walls. Still, I figured I'd rather be inside with the lizards than out with the lion."

Daddy asked, laughing, "Didn't you say you were going to be a zoo vet? I thought you'd like wild animals up close."

Rick laughed too. "Give me time to get used to it. I thought I was practically in the lion's mouth the last time he roared. I sat there with the lizards for what seemed like years. Finally I heard him grunting to himself farther off. Then I made a run for it."

Mom said, "You were probably safe enough close to the cabins. People are killed by lions sometimes if they walk alone in the bush at night."

"Well, I don't intend to get into a wild lion's space,"

Rick said. "Last night the walls of the outhouse actually jiggled when that lion roared. I felt like a fly in a stereo speaker."

We were still giggling when we got into the car to go look for animals.

A dusty, spicy smell came in through the car windows. The lion-colored grass was dotted all over with grey thornbushes. My eyes flicked over the bush, searching for any shape that meant animal.

"Do you think we can find the lions?" Rick asked.

"There!" Sandy interrupted. "Look, giraffes."

Their long necks showed above the thornbushes. Daddy drove closer. A big giraffe peered down at us from over a bush. His long lashes blinked over huge eyes.

Mom laughed and said, "God makes the strangest creatures."

I looked uneasily at Rick. What would he think of us talking about God? I couldn't tell if he had even heard what Mom said. He was leaning out his window taking a picture of the giraffe.

Suddenly the giraffe opened its mouth. A huge, long, purple tongue came out. It wrapped around a bunch of thorny leaves and slurped them back into the giraffe's mouth.

Rick swore softly. "Look at its tongue!" he blurted.

I'd heard people use God's name in vain before, but

never a member of my family. I looked at Daddy, wondering what he'd do.

"He can see it," Daddy said.

"Huh?" Rick said. He looked puzzled.

"God's name matters to us, Rick. He is our God," Daddy explained.

Rick turned bright red. "Oh, sorry."

I squirmed in my seat. It was bad enough having Rick swear, without Dad getting on his case. I looked back at the giraffe and burst out laughing. It was staring at us in a superior way, as if it was shocked at how we were acting.

Mom and Daddy and Rick were quiet after that. I couldn't tell if they were mad or what. I was glad there were animals to look at.

Once we saw elephants far away. Up close, we saw redgold impala. Their babies looked just like Bambi. Something scared the impala. They jumped across the road in huge graceful leaps. We saw four turkey-sized ground hornbills. They had huge beaks and movie-star eyelashes. One caught a lizard and banged it with its beak to kill it.

I kept looking at Rick. Was he mad at Daddy? Sandy talked twice as much as usual. It was like she was trying to fill in the quietness.

"Look! There's a waterbuck," she said, bouncing on

her seat and pointing out the window. "How come they have such long hair? Uncle Paul told me that their meat tastes terrible. How come they don't ever come in herds like impala? Impala are better. They can jump higher too. Did you ever see an impala before today, Rick?"

"Yeah, I had an old 1972 beater, but it couldn't jump very high," he answered, grinning. (Later on Daddy told me that Impala is also a kind of car.)

It was getting close to noon. The sun poured down. Even with the car windows wide open we were roasting. The shadows of the thorn trees looked like black puddles on the sun-bleached ground.

"There!" Mom said suddenly. "Ears! Under that bush."

"I see them! I see them!" Sandy said, bouncing on the seat. "It's lions!"

In the dark shadow under a thornbush, there were three pairs of round ears. Daddy drove closer. Another lion picked up its head. Three more stayed lying down flat. There were seven lions lying sprawled out like contented tomcats. One male that had only a little bit of mane reached out lazily and pawed at a lioness. She didn't even open her eyes. The lions looked contented and cuddly.

"I'd like to pet one," Mom said. "Don't they just look like they'd purr?"

We sat and watched. The only thing that moved were the flies on the lions' faces.

Rick chuckled and said, "They look laid back."

"This bunch won't move until it's cooler. I wouldn't mind getting out of the heat either," Daddy said. "We can come back and try to find the lions again this evening. Why don't we go to Kilaguni Lodge for lunch, and then to Mzima Springs?"

"All right!" Sandy and I both yelled together. We hardly ever got to go out to eat, and Kilaguni Lodge was neat.

Chapter
Two

~~~~~~~~~~~~~~~~~~~~

The inside of Kilaguni Lodge was air-conditioned. When we walked in, the cool air washed over me like water. It seemed dark inside after the bright sun. Big flagstones on the floor shone dimly.

"Hazel! Kevin!" a high voice called. I spun around to see a stranger heading toward us. She was tall and pretty. She came toward us, talking the whole way. "I didn't know you were here in Tsavo," she said. "Cliff and I came down two days ago."

She hugged Mom and shook hands with Dad. Then she looked at the rest of us. "So these are your girls. Hi!" She smiled at us. "Let's see. You must be Anika," she said, nodding at me, "and you're Sandy. You were at boarding school when I met your Mom and Dad. It's nice to meet you two."

I smiled back at her. She seemed nice. A man came up behind her and put his arm around her shoulders. He wasn't cute, but he had a friendly face. She looked at him and said, "This is my husband, Cliff."

He grinned and nodded at us.

"This is Rick Shaw," Dad said, introducing Rick. "He's a vet student from Oregon who is visiting with us."

I sighed with relief. I'd been holding my breath, wondering if Daddy was going to say who Rick was.

"He's really our brother," Sandy said, smiling happily. "Well, half brother anyway."

There was a dead silence.

Sandy looked at us, then ducked her head. Rick shuffled his feet. I could feel my face get hotter and hotter. Dad and Mom looked at each other. Daddy quirked one eyebrow up in a question. Mom nodded.

"With Hazel's permission, I'll explain," he said. "This isn't a secret, but it is awkward." Then he explained who Rick was. He told how Rick found us.

"Hazel and I have been praying for him ever since we came to know the Lord," he said, then turned to look at Rick. "Both of us are glad he's here."

Rick nodded uneasily.

Mr. Geisler reached out to shake Rick's hand. "Glad to meet you."

"Thanks," Rick said.

We went in to eat with them at the restaurant. The waiter came over to take our order. Everybody ordered the buffet. Then Rick said, "I'd love a cold beer. Have you got Budweiser?" Then he looked at us, shook his head twice quickly, and said, "Um, never mind. No beer. Um . . . how about a Coke?"

Mrs. Geisler had been asking me about school. She stopped when Rick ordered the beer. When Rick cancelled the order so quickly, Sandy and I giggled. Mrs. Geisler didn't. She had an odd look on her face.

I felt weird, too. It would have been better if Mrs. Geisler had said right out, "Your brother drinks!" Instead, it was like everyone was keeping a secret.

People talked. Rick even told some funny stories about vet school. It felt like a play, all fake. The Geislers went back to the buffet for dessert, and I followed them. As I came up behind them, I heard Mr. Geisler say, "His being here will hurt their witness for God. They can't possibly stay as—"

Mrs. Geisler poked him. He stopped talking in the middle of the sentence.

Until she poked him, I wasn't paying attention to what he said. Now I wondered if he was talking about Mom and Daddy. I sucked in my breath and tried to pretend I hadn't heard. *Not stay as what?* I wondered. My stomach went tight from worry. I didn't even feel like eating dessert, and it was trifle, my favorite.

We went out to the terrace after lunch. We could see the water hole where animals come to drink. After a fancy meal the British have cheese and biscuits. We ate ours out on the terrace. The biscuits are really crackers, and there were five or six different kinds of cheese. It was fun to cut off some cheese with the elegant silver knife.

Sandy flipped a cracker onto the low wall at the edge of the terrace, and an agama lizard with a bright-red head grabbed it. Three other lizards chased him. I took a bite of cheese and leaned back to watch. The cheese was smooth and tangy on my tongue. I ate a cracker slowly and wondered. Should I worry about what I'd heard the Geislers say?

I squinted out into the sunshine. There wasn't much moving by the water hole. I could see a herd of zebras. They were quite far away under the edge of the trees. Two tall marabou storks stood still near the water. Each was balanced on one long, light grey leg. Their black backs and white fronts made them look like ratty old men in tuxedos. They are scavengers. That means they eat dead things. Other times I'd seen them pulling off scraps of meat with their big pick-shaped beaks. Swallows were darting out over the water and around the lodge.

Suddenly one of the marabou storks snapped at a swallow that had come right by its head. The stork caught the swallow! The swallow's wings showed for a second, sticking out of the bigger bird's beak. Then the stork threw its head back and gulped at the swallow. It had to do it five times before it had the little bird completely down.

Rick swore and said, "Did you see that? That gooney bird just ate a swallow!"

He turned to look at us with his eyebrows high on his forehead.

"It did!" Sandy blurted. "It did! I saw it too."

I glanced uneasily at the Geislers, hoping they hadn't noticed Rick's swearing. One look told me they had. Mr. Geisler looked blank instead of friendly. Mrs. Geisler was looking down at her hands.

The Geislers left right after lunch. Since they were staying at Tsavo too, Mom had invited them over for breakfast tomorrow. Now I wondered if they'd come. They had seemed so nice.

After lunch we got in the car and drove toward Mzima Springs. Three Land Rovers passed us going really fast. Dust from the Land Rovers covered our car. When they went by us, I saw African men in the back of the Land Rovers. They had on green camouflage uniforms. Rifles stuck out of the back.

"Is there a war? Those men looked like the army to me," Rick asked, coughing at the dust.

"Not that I know of. It's probably just a small war." Daddy said.

"Kevin! Don't tease," Mom said, sounding irritated. "That was a poaching control unit."

"It looked military to me," Rick said insistently.

"It is, in a way. The units are trained like army units. They have to be to make any difference."

"Why?" Sandy asked.

"It's this way," Daddy explained. "Elephant tusks are worth a lot of money. At some point, people started looking at elephants as if they were walking treasure chests. Poor people, poor governments, and greedy politicians started killing the elephants. Even underpaid park rangers got involved in the killing. There are only one-tenth the number of elephants in Kenya now that there were in 1970."

Rick was nodding emphatically. "I've read about it. African elephants are on the endangered species list now. I remember reading that Kenya was doing something about it. So that military-looking bunch are an antipoaching unit. Good!"

"Why did the government change their mind?" Sandy asked. "Was it because they were afraid the tourists wouldn't come anymore?"

"That's right," Daddy said. "They needed the money from tourism. Besides that, countries that give Kenya money said they wouldn't help anymore unless the Kenyan government made the poaching stop."

"So they made the antipoaching units!" I said triumphantly. "Now the elephants are safe."

"Not always," Mom said. "Their tusks are still worth a lot of money. And there are plenty of places in the bush for the poachers to hide."

"Well, I hope they shoot all the poachers!" I said fiercely.

"Anika!" Mom said, but Rick was laughing.

"My bloodthirsty kid sister," he said, still chuckling. "I like elephants better than poachers too. I bet there wasn't much poaching here until you Christians came. Christianity tells people that they are boss of everything. Then they kill and take whatever they want."

My mouth dropped open. He was trying to blame everything on Christians!

Dad was talking, saying, "You sound very set against Christianity."

"See," Rick explained, "I'm really into the environment. That's why I'm in vet school. I don't want to work with tame animals that people rule. I want to work with the wild ones. For me it's like my religion. I want to be one with the trees and creatures. That's healthy. Christianity is different. It has a father-figure God who is a bossy ruler. It's the paternalistic religions with a domineering god that have let people wreck things. It's Christianity that told men to subdue the earth and dominate it. Before that, people lived as part of the whole, in harmony with nature."

I frowned in confusion. What did he mean? Half of the words didn't make sense to me. But I could tell that Rick had a different religion from ours. Besides, he thought Christianity was bad. I wanted to yell that he was wrong, but it was so confusing. I tried to shove the whole mess out of my head.

We'd been bumping down the road to Mzima Springs while we talked, and suddenly we were there.

The sun poured over me like warm syrup when I got out of the car. It was so strong it felt as if it had weight. I tipped my chin up and let it shine on my face. It laid warm fingers on my shut eyes. Sunshine always made me feel better inside.

Opening my eyes, I looked around. I could see doum palms with their fan-shaped leaves. Big, yellow-barked fever trees lifted their flat tops into the air. Quiet, dry, hot sky stretched out over the land. Signs on the path said Proceed at Your Own Risk. I guess they meant if we got bit by a crocodile, it was our own fault.

"Let's go to the tank! I want to see the fish!" Sandy said. She was hopping up and down at the edge of the path.

A group of little brown-grey vervet monkeys were in a tree by the path. We stopped to watch them. Two little kid monkeys were wrestling. They were the same size as miniature poodles. One let go and ran up a branch. The other chased it right out to the feathery leaves on the tip of the branch. A mother monkey had a tiny baby hugged to her tummy. It had a wrinkled face smaller than a walnut. A bigger monkey was sitting up like a man near the base of the tree. He looked bored and bossy.

"Hey, look," Rick said, laughing. "That monkey has bright blue—" He stopped and looked back at me and Sandy. Then he grinned and said, "Never mind. Anyway, I've got to get a picture of this."

Daddy frowned, and I giggled.

Sandy kicked me and whispered, "It's not funny. That was a gross thing to say!"

Mom glared at me, too. I managed to stop giggling for a few minutes, but every time I thought of what Rick said, I started again. Rick was really confusing me. I guess I'd always thought non-Christians were rotten people, or at least mixed-up like my cousin Tianna and her family. Rick didn't seem like that. He talked like Christians were the bad guys.

"Come on!" Sandy said, trying to make us hurry. "Come on, Rick! I'll show you the tank. It's awesome!"

On the way there we saw hippos on the far side of the water. All we could really see were little dark bumps on the water. The bumps were hippo eyes, noses, and ears.

"Whoosh!" Another hippo came up with a steamy snort. I could see it flip its ears to shake the water out. It floated with just its eyes, nose, and ears out like the others. One of the other hippos sank under the water. The heavy, green bush smelled of mud. We walked down to the tank.

The tank is a big box set down into the water. It has fingerprint-smeared glass on three sides and a bench in the back. Looking out into the water was like seeing into another world. A strange, clear, underwater room stretched out across the mud in front of us. Light flashed off the silver sides of barbel fish half as long as my arm. I looked far out to where the details blurred into a soft bluish fog. I couldn't see the hippos.

"Is the water ever clear!" Rick said.

"It comes underground down a lava tube all the way from the Chyulu Hills." Daddy said in his tour-guide voice.

"Once we saw a hippo underwater right by the tank." Sandy cut in excitedly. "It was the best! There was this huge animal sort of half swimming, half walking. Was it *ever* big. You know they are really dangerous. They bite people in half."

Rick looked at her with one black eyebrow up.

"They do!" Sandy insisted. "If you get in their way when they are walking at night they bite you in half!"

I cringed, wishing that Sandy would quit talking so much. Rick didn't seem to mind, though.

"Right in half?" he asked, laughing.

"Well, dead, anyway. Their teeth are this big." She held out her hands about a yard apart. "And they poke clear through you. It's true. Right, Dad?"

Daddy nodded and said, "Hippos are unpredictable. I wouldn't walk here at night while they are out of the water grazing."

"I don't care!" I said. "I think hippos are neat! I mean, they're so weird with their huge, flat, grass-mowing lips. I like the way they open their *enormous* mouths at each other when they play-fight."

"I'm not saying hippos are bad," Daddy said. "I don't think Sandy was either. God made them the way he wanted them. We just need to respect them to stay out of trouble."

Rick was watching Daddy with a puzzled look on his face. He suddenly asked, "And shoot them if they inconvenience you?"

"Some would look at it that way," Daddy said mildly.

"Not me!" I blurted, glaring at Daddy. He was going to make Rick think Christians really *were* bad guys.

Rick and Daddy both laughed, and we headed back for the car.

Chapter Three

Before dark we looked for the lions we'd seen sleeping. We looked again the next morning. We wanted to see them hunt. We never did find the lions, but something even better happened. Before breakfast we actually saw a leopard.

Mom was sitting in the front seat. Sandy volunteered to sit in the middle so that Rick could have a window in back. She was being so sweetsy-nice it made my teeth ache.

"There!" Mom suddenly said in a high, excited voice. "Kop, Stevin! Kop!"

Dad put on the brakes. "OK, I'm kopped now," he said, chuckling. "What is it?"

"It's a leopard! I just happened to glance up. There is a leopard in that acacia tree! I saw him go up the trunk!"

The car jerked as Daddy drove backwards. A second later we were under the tree, looking up. It *was* a leopard. He was standing on a branch, staring at us with savage, green eyes. There were patches of gold, early-morning sun across the tree branches. The leopard matched his background. The spots on his tawny hide made him blend in so much he was almost invisible.

Something sharp jabbed me in the ribs. "Ow! Sandy, back off," I hissed. Her hair was right in my face.

"But I can't see," she wailed. "Move over and give me room."

"Shhh!" Mom whispered. "Be still! You'll bother the leopard."

I scootched over and looked up at the leopard. For a second I couldn't find it. My eyes frantically searched the tree. "Hey, look!" I blurted. Then I remembered to be quiet. "He's got a kill!" I whispered. "It's the first wild leopard I've ever seen, and he's got a kill. See, it's where the branch he's on touches the trunk."

"Where?" Rick said. I looked over at him. He was leaning down toward my side of the car. He needed to look up out of my window to see the leopard.

"Move, Sandy," I said. "Give Rick a chance to look." Both of us ducked back and scootched down. Sandy, Rick, and I ended up stacked three-deep in front of the window. "The kill is there, right by the tree trunk." I whispered. "You can see a leg hanging down. I think maybe it's a wildebeest."

"Oh yeah! Awesome!" Rick whispered. Rick seemed

huge and strange that close to us. I could hear him breathing.

We all held still, watching. The car door felt cool and dusty on my cheek. The leopard took two steps toward us along the branch and hissed. He paused, then sat down, staring at us. That leopard was the most beautiful animal I'd ever seen.

"You want to pet that one?" Daddy asked quietly. He was teasing Mom because she'd said she wanted to pet the lions.

"No . . . I don't think so," Mom said thoughtfully. "There's something menacing about its eyes. It reminds me of Blake's poem about the tiger: 'Tiger, tiger burning bright in the forests of the night. What immortal hand or eye dare frame thy fearful symmetry.'"

"Praise him for what he has made," Daddy answered softly.

The leopard was nervous with us so near his kill. His tail twitched. He licked his back. Then he stretched and glared at us. Suddenly he paced down the branch and took a good grip on his kill. Then he yanked it out of the crotch of the tree. He turned and carefully backed down the tree. His shoulder and neck muscles slid under his sleek hide. On the ground he took a better grip of the kill. It was a wildebeest. You could tell it was heavy, but he trotted off quickly, dragging it between his front legs. His black ears were flat against his skull.

Everybody was quiet on the drive back to camp. It was like the leopard had hypnotized us. Just before we got there, Rick leaned forward to Mom and Daddy and said, "Your attitude toward animals puzzles me."

"Not what you expected?" Daddy asked.

"Do you believe differently than other Christians?" he asked. "You don't seem to think of animals as objects for people to do with as they like—or do you?"

"Killing the animals isn't Christians' fault," I interrupted. "Tell him!"

There was a long pause. Why didn't they answer? Was it because it *was* Christians' fault? I frowned. It couldn't be.

"Tell him!" I insisted again.

"It has to do with taking half the truth and not the whole of it," Mom said.

"Huh?" I asked, but we were pulling up behind our cabin, and the conversation stopped.

The Geislers did come to breakfast. They laughed and talked. Mr. Geisler's reddish blond mustache spread out across his face in the funniest way when he laughed. Still, things didn't feel right. I watched them, wondering.

"Tell them," Mrs. Geisler mouthed silently at her husband. I guess she thought nobody was looking at her.

He shook his head and mouthed, "Later."

Just then I saw a marabou stork walking in front of our cabin. It was inside the circle of white stones where you're allowed to walk. I got up and went toward it. The Geislers were making me nervous. Trying to see the stork close up was an excuse to get away from them.

Slowly and carefully, I walked up to the stork. It watched me. I got closer and closer. I could see its round yellow eyes. There were tiny black hairs sticking out of the bare red wrinkles on its neck. I took another step. It jerked its head and took off. Its huge black wings blew air across my face. The wind blew something across the ground by my foot. I jerked my foot back. It was one of those huge black ants that sting. My foot jerking made the ant fall into an antlion hole. I squatted down to watch.

My head was full of confused ideas as I watched the ant. What Rick had said about Christians and animals really confused me. Mom's answer hadn't helped at all. Besides, what was with the Geislers?

The ant was struggling to climb out of the cone-shaped antlion hole. Its black legs scrambled in the soft, dusty sides. I couldn't see the antlion. It was under the dust. But I could see what it was doing. It was flicking dirt onto the ant to make the ant lose its grip. See, if the ant lost its grip and slid to the bottom of the hole, the antlion would grab it and eat it. It didn't work, though. This ant was too big. It could reach to the top of the hole. The ant's front legs got a grip on a piece of grass. It pulled itself out and got away.

I felt with my finger in the bottom of the hole. My finger touched the round body of the antlion. I pinched him gently and picked him up. He was light brown and a little smaller than a grain of rice. He had big pincers. I dropped him. He dug a new hole by flicking the dust up with his head and backing in circles.

I smiled. God made such weird and neat things. I thought about Rick saying that he liked nature. It wouldn't be the same without knowing God. I could practically feel God smile at me. "Help Rick get to know you too," I prayed quietly.

I looked down at the antlion hole. I'd made that antlion do a whole lot of work just so I could watch him. Sort of to try and pay him, I found a smaller ant that didn't sting and dropped it into his hole. It scrambled frantically while the antlion flicked dirt at it. The antlion caught the ant in his pincers. He was dragging it under the dust when I heard Mom calling.

"Where on earth have you been?" Mom asked. "You knew we had to pack up and go right after breakfast. I don't know where you heave your lead sometimes!"

I giggled.

"Leave your head," Mom said carefully, correcting herself, then smiled. "The same place I leave mine, I guess. Get in there and get packed up!" She took a playful swat at me as I went through the door into Sandy's and my room.

"You have to do dishes tonight!" Sandy said as soon as I walked into the room. "I had to do breakfast dishes all by myself because of you."

"So?!" I said, starting to roll up my sleeping bag. "You don't have to brag about it, Goody-goody Two Shoes."

"Girls, be polite," Mom said. "Remember John 13:34. Practice it!"

I remembered John 13:34. It was that verse about people knowing we are Jesus' disciples by how we love each other. I sighed and finished rolling the sleeping bag. I didn't want to look at Sandy. She was being such a goody-goody. It wasn't fair. Still, I really did want to please Jesus. Finally I said, "Sorry, Sandy."

"It's OK," she said. "I forgive you."

That bugged me, too. It wasn't like she was perfect. She should say sorry, too. But to keep from getting mad again, I changed the subject.

"What was wrong with the Geislers?" I asked her.

One of her eyebrows went up like it did when she was surprised. "Nothing's wrong, is it? They're nice," she said. "Mrs. Geisler told me to call her Kim—not Aunt Kim, just Kim."

I shrugged. The words I'd overhead at Kilaguni Lodge ran through my head. *"His being here will hurt their witness. They can't possibly stay . . ."* I tried to stop my head from thinking about them.

Sandy interrupted my thoughts. "The Geislers are coming to Amboseli with us. They were going there anyway, same as us. Mom and Daddy asked if they wanted to drive with us."

"You sure?" I asked her. "The Geislers said they wanted to go with us?"

Amboseli is another game park. Mostly I like it even better than Tsavo. I knew we were going there today. I sighed. If the Geislers were coming with us they couldn't really be mad about Rick, could they?

We started late because the Geislers took so long to pack up. A bunch of guinea fowl ran along the road beside us for a few seconds. They looked like excited black footballs with chicken legs. We saw giraffe and gerenuk in the distance. It got hotter and hotter. I was tired of sitting in the bumping, hot, jerky, dusty car.

Rick suddenly swore.

My sweaty shirt stuck to the car seat for a second when I sat up to see what he was looking at. We'd just come up a steep hill. Now we were driving on the lava flow. I'd seen it before, and it really was weird. It looked like a huge, bare black river of twisted rock.

"I suppose you could call it hell," Daddy said to Rick. "It's the Shatani lava flow. *Shatani* means 'Satan' in Swahili."

"Hey, look," Rick said. "Sorry the language bugs you. It's gotten to be kind of a habit. I've been trying to remember, but it just slips out. I guess you'll just have to take me as I am, or leave me."

"We'll take you," Mom said, leaning over the backseat and squeezing his arm.

"Does that mean it's OK to swear?" Sandy blurted.

"Not for you," Rick answered, laughing.

"How can wrong and right be different for different people?" she insisted, sounding almost angry.

"It can't," Daddy said in a flat voice.

"But—," Sandy objected.

"We'll talk about this later," he said determinedly. Even Sandy knew it was no use arguing.

"Why don't we stop for a picnic lunch?" Mom asked, changing the subject. "That will give Rick a chance to look at the lava flow."

A few minutes later we drove down off the lava flow. We stopped in a kind of island of normal ground. The high sides of the lava flow were all around us. Dad parked the car under a tree. The Geislers pulled up next to us.

I was peeling a boiled egg when Daddy started his tour-guide speech. I looked at Rick, wondering if he would think it was dumb. I mean, sometimes it's embarrassing to have Daddy always explaining. Rick looked like he was really listening, so I relaxed and listened too. Daddy was explaining how the lava had poured out of the Chyulu Hills more than a hundred years ago. He explained so well I could almost see it gushing red-hot through its black, broken crust, lighting huge brushfires. No wonder the Africans thought it was something from Satan.

After lunch Daddy said, "Why don't you girls go explore the lava flow with Rick? We need to talk to the Geislers."

"All right!" Sandy yelled, grinning and hopping on one foot.

My heart did a double thump. I couldn't help feeling excited about exploring the Shatani lava flow. We'd never stopped long when we came here before. But on the way up the slope of the lava flow I looked back uneasily. What were Mom and Dad and the Geislers talking about? Whatever was going on had to be serious. Usually Mom wouldn't have let Sandy and me just go off out here in the wild.

Mom saw me look back and called, "Don't go far, and stay together. Be careful, that lava is sharp."

Up on the lava flow, heat blasted off the black rock into our faces.

"This place is as bare as the moon," Rick said, looking around.

"Look at this!" Sandy called from a few feet over. She'd found a place where the flow was as smooth as boiling hard candy. Rick bent down and touched a twisted bit of rock that stuck up. It came loose in his hands. He looked at it carefully, then dropped it into his pocket.

"Why're you keeping it?" Sandy asked.

"I dunno," he said. "Maybe I'll use it to keep me spiritually in tune. It can help me focus for meditation. Kind of like a crystal or a mantra."

"What's a mantra?" I asked.

"It's something that helps a person tune in to meditate. It helps you get spiritually in touch with the whole, the oneness of everything," he said.

"Like praying?" asked Sandy.

"Only I'm not talking to a dominant father-God like you do. It's just communing with everything there is. There isn't a boss. Nobody is my boss but me."

I frowned and blurted, "There is! He made it, all of it." If there was one thing I knew for sure, I knew God was the Creator. I'd felt him loving me through his creation too many times to be confused about that. I waved my arms toward everything around us and said, "It's *way* too beautiful to be an accident!"

Rick didn't answer. He just shrugged and started hunting around for other pieces of rock. I started looking too. So did Sandy. Sandy and I automatically kicked at the rock first to make sure there were no snakes or scorpions underneath. Twice, skinks shot out, making me jump. But I knew those sleek lizards didn't hurt anything but bugs.

I found one piece of lava that looked like a piece of wood. On top of it was another blob of rock. It was interesting looking. *I'm keeping it,* I thought. I could feel the heat of the black rock on my hand.

I'm not going to use it for a mantra, whatever that is, I told myself. *I just want this one because it's pretty.* I thought for a minute. *And because I like the neat things God makes.*

My piece of lava looked like a frog on a log. It felt sharp and heavy. I knew I'd have to be careful how I held it or I could cut myself.

Sandy came up behind me. "Where's Rick?" she asked, looking worried.

I stood up straight to look around. I couldn't see him.

"We're not supposed to be by ourselves," she said. "What if there's a leopard?" She bit her knuckle the way she always does when she's scared.

"It would run, like the one did this morning," I said to make myself feel braver. Then I yelled, "Rick!"

"I don't care, I'm going back," Sandy said.

"Don't tell that he left us," I said. "I'll find Rick and come back too, OK?"

When I had yelled, it had sounded loud. I was afraid I might bother something I didn't want to bother, so I didn't yell again. I just started walking instead, looking for Rick. I heard rocks clinking on the slope. I froze. What if it wasn't Rick that was there? What if it was some animal?

Chapter Four

"Rick?" I tried to call. It came out in a croak. *This is stupid,* I thought to myself. *If it isn't Rick that I hear, it's probably just a baboon.* Still, I couldn't make my mouth open to call again. I edged sideways and looked down the side of the lava flow. My breath came out in a *whoosh* of relief. It was Rick.

I stared at what he was doing. He was picking through the broken rock on the slope with his hands.

"Don't!" I yelled, going as fast as I could down the rough slope. "Don't put your hands down in the rock!"

Rick looked at me like I was crazy. His eyebrows were straight and level over blue eyes.

"There's poison snakes and stuff!" I said. The way he was looking at me made me feel stupid. I stopped partway down the slope. "Really," I said. "You could get bit. There are even scorpions."

He looked at me hard. "You're not fooling, are you?"

I shook my head.

After a minute he said, "Thanks for warning me."

He started walking up toward me. A small red-brown blur shot out from under the rocks almost at his feet. He jumped and stumbled onto one knee. The blur was a mongoose. A second one streaked after it. The weasely little animals ran a little way. They stopped on top of a rock, sat up like dogs begging, and yelled at us.

Rick got back onto his feet, laughing. "This place is full of life. I love it," he said. "But if you can't put your hands into the rocks, how did you get that?" He made a motion to the chunk of rock I was carrying.

"Well, I sort of kicked it over first to make sure there wasn't anything under it. Besides, it wasn't where there were so many rocks jumbled together. There's too many hiding places here. Some places we just stay out of."

I held the rock out to him. "Isn't it a neat one? See, that blob on it looks kind of like a frog."

He took it and looked it over. "It is neat. It has a different mental feel to it than the one I've got. It forms my thoughts in different patterns."

"You can have it," I said. "I can always find a different one another time." Suddenly I was worried. If I gave it to him, was I helping him do his religion? I blurted, "You have to think about the only real God sometimes when you look at it, OK? I mean, he loves us. He made everything, and it is so neat . . . " I paused, feeling silly, and added, "He loves me anyway. It's kind of hard to explain."

Rick was looking at me with one eyebrow up. I tried again to explain, "Like that giraffe looking at me and making me laugh. When I remember to look, God's love is all over the place smiling at me. Besides, he came down and died for us. He did it to take the punishment for wrong things so we could be his kids. He helps me all the time. It's true! Really! Here." I held out the rock. "Take it."

Rick reached out and took the rock. "Thanks," he said, smiling. "I don't know about this father-God stuff, but you're OK, Sis."

I smiled. It was the first time I felt like we could be friends. We walked back together not saying anything. It was a friendly kind of quiet. The heat came through the bottom of my shoes as we walked across the black lava. I looked down. My runners were scuffed and cut from the rock. I glanced over to see if Rick's shoes were the same and gasped. Rick's leg was all scraped. It was bleeding into his sock.

"Hey, you cut your leg!" I blurted.

He nodded, "Bumped some lava when the mongoose scared me. It's no big deal. Better than a snake bite," he laughed.

We were most of the way back to the car when I saw Sandy. She was standing, frozen, with her back to us.

"Sandy!" I called. "What are you doing?"

"*Shhh!*" she said, and ran toward me. She grabbed my arm and started whispering frantically. "You can't go down. They're arguing. The Geislers are arguing with Mom and Daddy."

We stood still and listened. Weaverbirds in a tree behind us were making a racket. Mrs. Geisler's voice was so loud it cut right through the noise. She was almost yelling as she said, ". . . and I feel that you should resign from the mission. This situation ruins any chance we have of modeling a healthy Christian family pattern to the African church!"

"As I said before," Daddy said, sounding patient, "why don't we leave that decision up to the mission and the church?"

I bit my lip and glanced at Rick. His black eyebrows were down in a furious frown. The muscles at the corners of his jaw were bulging.

Mr. Geisler's voice said, "If you won't listen, we'll have to go to the field representative about this. Kim and I feel very strongly that having an illegitimate child here will ruin your ministry. It is—"

Rick snorted explosively and strode forward. I stumbled after him, practically running. Sandy was right behind me.

As we burst in on them Daddy was saying, "Feel free to do that. The mission was not ignorant—"

"I don't know who you people think you are!" Rick bellowed, striding angrily toward the Geislers. His hands were balled into fists. "This is absolutely none of your business!"

There was a moment of frozen stillness. I could hear the weaverbirds chattering. My throat was so tight it hurt. I could see that Mom had been crying.

Rick glanced at her, clenching and unclenching his fists. "Look," he said, turning to the Geislers, "you people call yourselves Christians. You say you follow God's ways. If this is how your God wants you to act, I don't think much of him or of his uncaring rules."

Mrs. Geisler moved closer to her husband. She looked like she wanted to cry. "It isn't that way," she said desperately.

"I think we'd better go, Kim," Mr. Geisler said. They walked toward their car. Just before he opened their car door he said, "We will be praying for you. I know this isn't easy."

"We'll be praying for you, too," Mom called after them in a shaky voice.

Their car disappeared down the dusty road and left us standing there.

"Are they still going to Amboseli?" I asked.

"I don't know," Daddy said in a tired voice. "We'd better get going. Rick, I'm sorry things got so unpleasant.

It isn't as simple as it looks. Kim and Clifford don't dislike us. This is painful to them too. We just disagree on some things. With help it can be worked out."

Rick made a snorting noise. "They think you should quit your job because of me. If that's Christianity, count me out!" He got into our car and slammed the door.

Nobody said anything in the car. I wanted to talk to Mom and Daddy about what was happening with the Geislers, but I didn't dare with Rick there.

After a long, hot time, I noticed Daddy was slowing down. There was noise outside the car. I jerked awake and stared out the window. There was a mob of Masai people in the road. They were crowded around another car. High, angry voices shrilled in the hot air. Some of the kids were stooping to pick up rocks. A young man with a red cloth tied over one shoulder was shaking his spear at the car. More people were running toward the road from a *manyatta*. A *manyatta* is a Masai village. I could see the thorn wall and the tops of the mud sleeping shelters through the bush.

"It's Geislers' car!" Mom said suddenly.

Daddy frowned and got out of our car.

"Kevin, be careful!" Mom called after him.

"Why should we help people who are such jerks?" Rick asked, sounding frustrated. Mom looked at him, but she didn't answer his question. Instead, she turned around to Sandy and me and said, "Let's pray that God will give your wather fisdom."

I felt so tense inside that Mom's mistake made me giggle even more than usual. Mom said, "Seriously, kids, this could be dangerous. Probably the Geislers didn't pay for taking pictures and the Masai are angry. That *manyatta* isn't rich. They go to a lot of trouble to be here by the road dancing for tourists. They've even dragged rocks onto the road to get people to slow down and look."

I suddenly remembered something Uncle Paul told us. A tourist van had hit a Masai boy. See, the boy didn't know cars can't stop instantly. He had jumped right in front of the van to make it stop. The van didn't dare stop after the boy was hurt. The whole village thought the driver had done it on purpose. The driver kept on going and went and told the police what happened. The next morning when the van driver went to fill up with gas, he found the boy's father waiting for him. The father had walked all night to get vengeance. He killed the van driver.

Suddenly I felt like praying. I asked God to let Daddy explain things well. That way everybody would understand and not be angry. I rolled down my window to listen. The Masai still sounded angry, and now they were crowding around Daddy.

"Fool man," Rick grunted. Then he got out of the car and went to stand close beside Daddy.

"Why'd he get out?" Sandy asked. Her voice sounded scared. "He's mad at the Geislers."

"I think he's trying to protect your father," Mom answered. She sounded like she wasn't sure if she should laugh or cry.

I leaned out the window, listening. The people had quieted down. Daddy was saying he would pay for the pictures the Geislers took. He said the Geislers were new guests in Kenya and did not understand. The whole group gathered around him and Rick. Rick looked nervous. When Dad asked for one person who could give out the money, about ten reached for it. All of them were yelling. Each one was trying to get Daddy's attention. They each were trying to convince Daddy to give the money to them.

Daddy yelled, *"Basi, basi!"* which means, "Stop!" Then he said, "If you cause trouble here, the police will not allow you to do this, and you will become poor." He asked for an elder who would distribute the money fairly. They argued with each other for a few seconds, then a boy ran off toward the *manyatta*. We waited.

We kept waiting. It was hot. The brownish grey flies were everywhere. I begged to get out of the hot car. Mom wouldn't let me.

I could tell Dad was getting impatient. He looked very irritated. Finally a whole bunch more people came walking from the *manyatta*. An old man was in the center of the group.

"I hope Dad remembers to be polite," Mom said nervously as they approached him and Rick. Mr. Geisler was with them now, too. The elder looked very dignified. He greeted Daddy. Daddy greeted him, asking in Swahili how he was, how his family was, how the land was, and the cattle. That's the polite way to do things there.

The elder asked Daddy questions, too. Dad explained about our family. Then he said that the Geislers had done the wrong thing because they were new in Kenya. It took a long time. It's not polite to hurry.

Finally the elder accepted money from Mr. Geisler. People had crowded close to listen. One of the men said something angrily, but the elder made him be still. Then he turned to the crowd. He made a long speech about how they should be polite to guests. I knew what he said because he did it in Swahili. I guess he spoke in Swahili instead of Masai so that Daddy would see that things were being done properly. I squirmed and watched a fly crawl on the elder's face.

Rick had come back. He leaned back against the car with his arms crossed. His eyes were watching the Masai. I saw him look at a *moran*—that's what the young men who are warriors are called. He looked at the old women with their shaved heads and big beaded earrings.

Finally the speech was done. Daddy walked over toward us. Rick stood up and said, "I'd really like some pictures of these people if you think it's safe. I'll pay, of course."

The elder smiled when Daddy asked him. Mom let us get out of the car. I stretched, glad to be out in the action finally. Warm sun and the strong smell of dry cow dung from the *manyatta* surrounded me.

Some of the Masai girls ran together and started dancing. They wanted Rick to take their picture. Dust spurted from under the dancers' feet. They sang in high, shrill voices. Their shoulders, hips, and hands jerked in time to a complicated rhythm. I grinned. Africa was full of the best stuff!

Before Rick had finished getting his camera out, both of the Geislers came over. "Thanks for saving our hide!" Mr. Geisler said, wide-eyed. "I thought we were going to get lynched for a second there. Why so much fuss about paying for pictures?"

All the time Daddy was explaining, neither of the Geislers would look at Rick. They didn't even look at him when he said something. Finally they got in their car and left. Rick stared after them, frowning. Then he went to take pictures of the dancers.

The *moran* who had shaken his spear at the Geislers

walked over near the line of dancers. He stood balanced on one leg holding a long spear. The other foot was resting on the knee of the leg he stood on. The red cloth he wore outlined his sleek body. He looked proud and wild like an eagle.

"Will you take a picture of me with him?" Rick asked Daddy. "Ask him politely. He doesn't look like a good man to offend."

Daddy laughed, "You'll have to pay him, of course."

Next to the sleek *moran,* Rick looked big and pale. Rick shook the *moran*'s hand and paid him. Then Rick said, "I will be a warrior, too." He tried to copy the way the *moran* had been standing earlier. Rick couldn't do it. He couldn't balance on one leg with the other resting on his knee. The little Masai kids shrieked with laughter, and even the warrior smiled.

When we drove off, the Masai smiled and waved. Little kids ran after our car, screeching and smiling.

Sandy stared back at them, wide-eyed. She turned around and said, "Now I know why we never stop!"

Daddy said, "Sometimes I think I'll never really have the patience I need to live in this country."

"Hey, man, you did great!" Rick said. "After we got things straightened out, things were cool. I liked the old man and that guy about my age. Did you call him a moron?"

We all laughed and Mom said, "No, mor*an*. It means 'warrior.' Anyway, we should thank God that we're safe."

I knew she meant that we should pray, but Rick didn't know that. He butted right in to ask more questions about the Masai.

I watched out the window, only half listening, while Daddy talked.

"Most of them still live the old way. They were a wandering warrior people who kept cattle. They lived on milk and blood from their cattle. They loved the cattle more than anything. No boy was considered a man until he had killed a lion or a man. They were so good at fighting that the slave traders didn't dare come into Kenya. When other tribes started wearing our kind of clothes and going to school, most of the Masai refused. The few that did go to school often did well. It's only recently that they've been sending more of their children to school."

"You'll see more of them in Amboseli Park," Mom said. "They're allowed to graze their cattle in the park."

"Are they poachers?" Rick asked.

"Not that I've heard of," Daddy said. "In fact, they probably keep poachers out. They don't like other people on their land. The elephant herds are healthier in Amboseli."

It was late afternoon by the time we got into

Amboseli National Park. Kilimanjaro, Africa's highest mountain, is near Amboseli. It's so huge it fills up a whole section of the sky. Right then we couldn't see anything except the bottom of the mountain. The rest was under the clouds. Nearly every day Kilimanjaro makes itself a new cloud blanket.

Tsavo, the park we'd just left, was different from Amboseli. Tsavo was wide, hot, dusty, and wild. It didn't have any center. Amboseli does. The heart of Amboseli is a huge swamp.

After we came into Amboseli we saw zebra, wildebeest, and little gold-and-black Thomson's gazelle. We saw a secretary bird stalking through the grass, looking for snakes to eat. Daddy wouldn't stop. We were coming up on the eastern edge of a new part of the swamp when I saw them.

"Elephants!" I yelled, pointing. I could see two grey backs over the thick thornbushes.

"Where?" Mom asked, craning to see.

"There!" Rick said. "There by that big yellow-barked tree."

I looked for the tree, and there were more elephants.

"One, two, three . . . ," Sandy counted. "There's ten of them!"

Daddy had slowed down, but he still wouldn't stop.

"Can't we stop?" I pleaded. "Just for a second?" In

Amboseli cars aren't allowed to go off the roads. The tourists were following the big cats around so much that the cats couldn't hunt except at night. It made it hard for the lions. Some of the cheetahs died, so the park made a rule not to go off the roads. I knew we couldn't drive over closer to the elephants.

"There will be more elephants tomorrow," Daddy said. "We still have to register, get set up, and make our supper."

"Please?" Sandy broke in. "Rick hasn't seen any wild elephants up close yet."

"Never mind me," Rick said. "Besides, isn't that group going to cross the road?"

It was, too. There were three of them coming toward the other elephants. Daddy would have to stop now, with elephants right on the road.

Chapter
Five

~~~~~~~~~~

The biggest elephant was in front. It paced slowly and gracefully toward us. One huge front foot swung forward. The foot got way wider when the elephant stepped down. I could hear a quiet scuffing sound. My insides suddenly jiggled and the car seemed to vibrate a little. All three elephants swung around.

"Oh, cuuuute!" Sandy said.

There was a baby elephant trailing behind. The elephants hurried back to the baby. My insides jiggled again.

"Did you feel that?" I asked.

Nobody answered. I shrugged. I was probably imagining the jiggling. How could elephants jiggle my insides, anyway?

The baby was with its mother now. He was leaning up against her while she stroked him with her trunk. He looked tired. His little round ears drooped.

"Look at the fuzzy hair on its back," Mom said softly.

The big elephant looped her trunk around him and hugged him tight under her. She put one front leg a little forward. Then I saw her teats, there between her front legs. She was trying to get him to suck. He tried a bit. Then he quit and leaned against his mom. I wondered, *Is there something wrong with him?*

After a minute the elephants started moving again. When they crossed the road in front of us, one of the middle-sized elephants seemed to be trying to help the baby. That's when I saw.

"Look, the baby *is* hurt!" I blurted. "It's limping! Something is wrong with its back leg." It hurt me to watch it limp tiredly after its mother. I spun toward Rick and said, "You're going to be a vet, can you tell?"

He was watching the baby, frowning. "Hip dislocated?" he said, not sounding sure. The baby was dragging its left back leg.

Just then the other elephants saw the big elephant coming. Three hurried over. The way they touched each other with their trunks, you could tell they were glad to see each other. As soon as its mother stopped, the little elephant lay down flat underneath her to rest.

I watched it lie there, and I felt terrible! That leg probably really hurt. "We've got to get somebody to help it!" I blurted. "We've got to."

"Anika," Mom said. "I know how you feel, and I'm sorry. But I don't think anybody can help. It's a wild animal."

"They *have* to!" I insisted. "Look how tired it is." I thought about leaving the little elephant to hurt and hurt. My throat got tight with panic. "It's not fair!" I yelled.

"You're right. It's not fair. But things won't be fair until Jesus comes back and all creation is free of the suffering from sin," Mom said. "We fight the suffering when we can. But I don't see how we could possibly do anything about this."

"You just don't care!" I said, sticking my chin up. "You just don't want to do anything about it!"

"Settle down!" Daddy said. "That's enough."

I crossed my arms and shoved myself back into the corner of the seat. I frowned and tried hard not to cry. Getting mad always made me feel horrible. I felt terrible for yelling at Mom. I felt even worse about the baby elephant hurting. I glanced at Rick. The way Mom and Dad acted, no wonder he thought Christians didn't care. I didn't even look up when a whole troop of baboons crossed the road.

When we were driving up to our cabin I suddenly remembered Dr. Field.

"We can tell Dr. Field!" I blurted. Everybody was getting out of the car. I didn't budge.

"What, Anika?" Mom asked, sticking her head back in to look at me.

"We can drive and find Dr. Field and tell him. You know. He's that American scientist man that came up to our school once. Like, he studies how animals talk. He said he was going to start working on elephant talk. He said he'd start by working with that lady who studies elephants in Amboseli. So he's here, see. He's nice. We can go find him now. We'll tell him, and—"

"Anika," Daddy said, cutting in. "Stop sulking about that elephant. There's a lot of work to do right now. Get out of the car and get busy. If you must, we can talk about the elephant later. Mom already told you, it probably can't be helped."

Usually family devotions is our time to talk. Rick wasn't there. He'd gone to his room, saying he wanted to write in his journal. I frowned at Daddy, who was reading the Bible to us. Rick probably didn't want to hear us talking about God. Already he thought Christians didn't care about nature. Mom and Daddy wouldn't even help with the baby elephant.

"Dad," Sandy said, interrupting, "how come it seems like you think it's OK for Rick to swear? I don't get it. Swearing is wrong, right?"

"Right, swearing is wrong," Daddy said, smiling. "It's wrong all the time for anyone to use God's name in vain. It's also wrong to use coarse words for body functions. God made us in his image, and it dishonors him and us to use filthy language. *But,* Rick doesn't know Jesus. It's not proper for us to try to force God's rules on him before he knows God's love. While we were *still* sinners, Jesus died for us."

"Still, we shouldn't let him think God is bad!" I blurted angrily. "When he said Christians treat animals like things, you didn't even argue. All you said was something about half the truth and not all of it. That doesn't even make sense!"

"It's complicated," Mom said. "The Bible teaches the truth, that people are shepherds of nature. That means we are in charge of it for God. God is the real boss. When he made things, he said they were good. He wants us to take good care of the things he created on earth. But people got greedy. They only wanted to remember that they were in charge. They didn't want to remember that God is really boss."

"Oh, I get it," I said. "The half of the truth they wanted to keep was that they were in charge of nature. Now people even say they own it. So then they think it's OK to ruin it if they want to get something like gold or whatever."

Daddy nodded and said, "That's why what Rick says is partly true."

"So we have to help the baby elephant to show him he is wrong!" I said triumphantly.

"Anika," Mom said, sounding tired, "we can't bother busy scientists about a hurt wild animal. I'm almost certain it can't be helped anyway."

"We can!" I said desperately. "They're studying the elephants. They care, even if you don't!"

"Look," Daddy said, "I don't like your tone of voice. If they are studying these elephants they almost certainly already know about the baby. Now that's enough!"

I bit my lip, thinking it was no use talking to them. They just didn't care.

That night I couldn't go to sleep. I frowned in the dark. Well, if Mom and Daddy didn't care, I did. God told us to take care of creation and that included baby elephants. I knew that God also wanted me to listen to my parents, but I shut that out of my head.

"Anika?" Sandy whispered.

I pretended to be asleep. She called twice more, then was quiet.

I turned over. Every time I shut my eyes I saw that poor, tired baby elephant. I remembered that Mom had said that she and Dad fight the suffering when they can. *Yeah, sure!* I thought angrily, *but they won't even do anything to help the baby elephant.*

I clenched my teeth. *I'll go tell Dr. Field myself,* I thought fiercely. *I'll get up early before anyone else. I'll walk to the gas station down the road and make some-*

one take me to Dr. Field. I'll show Rick that Christians care.

I was way too mad to pray. That should have warned me right then. Anytime I'm too mad to pray, it seems like I end up doing something stupid.

When I was almost asleep, I suddenly remembered what the Geislers had said. A sick feeling washed over me. Daddy had said they'd gone to mission headquarters. I bit my lip. Could they really get Mom and Daddy kicked out of the mission? I shook my head and turned over. I couldn't fix the thing with the Geislers. The baby elephant was different. "I will help him. I will!" I whispered as I dropped off to sleep.

Sometimes I can wake up when I tell myself to. It worked that morning. It was dark in the cabin, but when I looked out, the sky was dim grey in the east.

The baby elephant, I thought, and I shivered. I'd never just gone off on my own before in the game park. I knew that this was wild, dangerous country. "I don't care!" I whispered and got out of bed. My knees quivered when I stood on one foot to pull my shorts on.

A few minutes later I was walking down the road behind the cabins. I smiled a wide smile. I was actually doing it! I was going to get help for that baby elephant. Cool wind stroked my cheeks. The air was full of birdsong. Kilimanjaro hadn't made its cloud hat yet.

The smooth, snowy top shone pink where the sun touched it. The dust came over my thongs when I stepped into the soft powdery places on the road. It felt cool on my feet. All of the earth was singing a wild psalm of praise to God.

I spun in a circle, throwing my hands out to the beautiful morning. Then I stopped. What would Mom and Daddy think when they found out I was gone? What if they thought a lion got me? I should have left them a note at least. I bit my lip, suddenly wanting to go back.

"What about the baby elephant?" I whispered to myself fiercely. "How do you think he feels?" I thought of how he had looked leaning tiredly against his mother. *I will help him!* I thought and kept on walking.

There were African men at the filling station. They were putting fuel into the zebra-striped minivans that the tourists rent. I hesitated. Would one of them really take me to Dr. Field? Suddenly I was afraid to ask. *Those men are busy. Besides, they'd probably just make me go back,* I thought. *Well, I won't go back!*

I walked quickly past on the other side of the road. A couple of vervet monkeys in the big trees there chattered at me. A few minutes later I was out in the grasslands on the road to Amboseli Lodge. My insides quivered with fear. I knew perfectly well that no one was supposed to walk alone in the game park.

Still, it was exciting. I'd always wanted to walk so I could really touch, hear, and smell things. "Amboseli Lodge isn't *too* far," I told myself. "I'll get someone there to take me to Dr. Field."

Gold sunlight washed down across me. My shadow stretched across the dusty grass. I stuck my chin up and tried to look like an explorer. Explorers had walked all across Africa. A little Thomson's gazelle flicked its tail and trotted away.

"Nhuh-nhuh!" something grunted. I jumped, but it was only a zebra. Their sound is like the beginning of a horse's nicker. Three of them were standing in a row staring at me. There were more zebras and some wildebeests behind them.

Suddenly a wildebeest went into a wild dance. They do that sometimes. I couldn't help grinning, watching this one. Another joined it, then another. Wildebeest are goofy-looking gazelles. They're brown-grey with a scraggy mane like a horse. Now these three were kicking high, twisting like broncos, acting like they'd suddenly gone crazy with joy.

When I looked down the road again, I could see elephants. I froze. They had come out of a patch of bush. If I kept going they would see me. I stood still, almost holding my breath. What did explorers do with elephants?

The elephants *were* coming toward me. I felt bare and small in all that open space. There was nowhere to hide. If I even moved they'd see me for sure. I crouched down, making myself as small as I could.

Maybe they won't care even if they do see me, I told myself. I hugged my knees, trying to make myself smaller. I wished I was beside some cows so I'd look like a Masai herd boy to the elephants. I knew that animals are nervous about things they're not used to. Somehow I didn't think these elephants would be used to a twelve-year-old white kid walking around by herself.

The elephants were closer now. They swung steadily along, obviously going somewhere. The one in front had a notch in her ear. She swung her trunk back and forth along the ground as she walked. They loomed bigger and bigger. Elephants had never seemed this huge when I watched them from the car. I could see the pattern of skin wrinkles on the front elephant's forehead. She was heading a little to my left.

I held still and prayed in my head, *Please God, these are your elephants. . . .*

I didn't get any farther. A half-grown elephant suddenly lifted his trunk and swung toward me. He froze, ears out, trunk up, sniffing and listening. He squealed. The whole bunch whirled toward me. Their raised trunks and wide ears made them look even bigger. My insides ached, and the back of my throat tasted like vomit.

After a long minute, the big lead elephant put down her trunk. She started walking again, but she turned a little to the left to go by me. Most of the herd followed her. The one that smelled me first didn't go. He was still staring at me. It was a half-grown boy elephant. He wasn't very big for an African elephant. Still, he was way too big for me. Now he snorted at me and flapped his ears. He took two shuffling steps toward me, kicking up dust. Then he watched to see if anything would happen.

"Go away!" I whispered. "Go on. Get!"

I was still crouched on my heels. Desperately, I hugged my knees tighter. One foot skidded out from under me. My behind hit the dust with a bump.

The boy elephant's ears fanned out in surprise. He squealed and hurried off toward the herd. He tucked his behind underneath him. He was in a hurry to get away from the strange thing on the road. I sat there in the dust, laughing with relief. The little elephant wasn't as tough as he thought, and I knew just how he felt. I didn't feel like an explorer any more at all. I sighed and stood up on shaky legs.

"This is stupid," I said, right out loud. "I'm going back."

That's when I heard the van. It was coming fast, kicking up dust. I moved off the road and waved frantically.

It stopped so fast that gravel skidded under its wheels. The driver leaned out the window, frowning, and said, "Walking in the park is not permitted. Get in. I will take you to Amboseli Lodge."

"But my family is at the Ol Tukai *banda*s," I retorted.

"I will take you to Amboseli Lodge!" the driver insisted, frowning furiously. "I must pick up the tourists there. If I am late, I have lost my job!"

I got in. The van started before I had the door shut. I landed with a thud in the seat. The van rocked from side to side as we shot down the road. I clutched at the seat to keep my balance and stared at the driver. *He must be really scared about losing his job,* I thought. The van leapt over a huge bump, and my head touched the ceiling.

A few seconds later we stopped in front of Amboseli Lodge. The driver practically pushed me out the door.

"It is forbidden to walk in the park!" he called after me. The van's tires squealed. It raced across the parking lot and stopped by a group of tourists.

What's going to happen to me now? I wondered.

Chapter
Six

I stood there watching tourists get into the van. I bit my lip. I was at Amboseli Lodge. Now what would happen?

Someone chuckled behind me. An English voice said, "That driver got rid of you in a hurry."

I spun to look. A woman in a skirt and a loose blouse was standing there. She was no tourist. She had the kind of tan you only get from spending hours and hours in the sun. Her short, blonde hair was dry and sun-bleached. Suddenly I realized I was staring and ducked my head.

"What's the matter?" she asked. "Cat got your tongue?"

"Um . . . no," I said, glancing at her uneasily. Her eyes were laughing. There were lots of smile wrinkles on her face. Still, she didn't look like the kind of person who'd let you get away with anything.

"Actually, I didn't even want to be here," I blurted, feeling flustered. "I was trying to get to Dr. Field. See, I have to talk to him about an elephant."

"About an elephant?" she asked with both eyebrows up. "For that you set out walking? That driver found you walking, didn't he?"

I ducked my head. Why had I said anything about the elephant anyway? That was dumb. My mouth felt dry. I swallowed, trying to get the courage to explain that I only wanted to get back to my family now. I knew going back was the right thing to do.

"An important personal matter concerning an elephant, is it?" she said, interrupting my thoughts. "Well, that can be managed. I know where Bruce Field is, and as I'm nearly finished with my business here I'll give you a lift. I wouldn't mind hearing what sort of urgent message concerning an elephant could bring a girl like you out on her own. I'll meet you here in ten minutes."

She spun on her heel with a swirl of skirts and disappeared into the lodge. I stared after her. She was actually going to take me to Dr. Field! My heart thudded in my throat. I knew I should go back. Still . . . if she would take me to Dr. Field . . . I frowned. I was stuck now, wasn't I? It would be rude to back out now and ask for a ride home, wouldn't it? I squirmed, trying to convince myself I couldn't back out.

When she came back, I just went with her in her Range Rover. She didn't say anything. Everything I could think of saying or asking sounded stupid to me. I looked around uneasily. There was all kinds of odd gear around. There was a two-way radio stuck to the dash, and on top of it was a three-ring binder.

The binder was open. I leaned forward to see better. I could see two big pictures of elephants. The Range Rover rocked over some bumps and the binder fell off the dash. I picked it up quickly and tried to open it to the same place. The whole binder was full of photographs. Each one was of a different elephant.

"You're the elephant lady!" I blurted, then added, "Um . . . I mean, the lady who studies elephants."

She laughed. "Yes," she said, "I'm Margaret Webb. I don't mind being called an elephant lady as long as you aren't referring to my size."

"I can tell you, then!" I blurted. "See, yesterday when we were driving in, we were passing this swamp. We were late because we had to stop the Masai from stoning the Geislers' car. Daddy helped even though the Geislers were mad at Mom and Dad because of my half brother." I stopped and frowned. I wasn't making sense. That made me even more flustered. "Like, see, Rick was adopted, and he thinks everything is Christians' fault, with the environment, you know—"

Dr. Webb interrupted, "Hold up. Take a deep breath and compose yourself."

I could tell she was trying not to laugh. That made me feel even sillier.

"We're nearly to camp," she said. "When we get there, you're most welcome to tell your tale. Only do try to stick to the point. It was about an elephant, was it not? Though I find prodigal half brothers and angry Masai intriguing, I doubt if they are central to our current concerns."

I bit my cheek. *Me and my big mouth,* I thought. *Why did I have to drag Rick into this? Why couldn't I just have stayed home?*

She turned the wheel. We bounced off the road onto a dirt track. A man was stepping out of a camper. She yanked the parking brake on and climbed out. "Bruce, there's a young lady here to see you about an urgent matter concerning an elephant."

I wished I could disappear. What came next didn't help. Dr. Webb turned toward me and said, "I've just had a thought. Child, do your parents know where you are?"

I shook my head, wishing even harder to disappear.

"Oh, for Pete's sake!" she said. "I'll give the park office a shout on the wireless. You find out what brought this child out, Bruce." She turned toward me, "Just where are your parents?"

"The Ol Tukai *banda*s," I said with my head down. She left.

"Well?" Dr. Field asked, stopping in front of me. "What can I do to help you?"

I looked up at him. He was tall and had a scraggly red beard. At first I was afraid, but then I looked at his eyes. They were brown and kind. I swallowed hard. This time I was determined not to tell about Rick and the Geislers. I would only tell about the baby elephant.

I finished by saying, "And Rick thinks it's got a dislocated hip. He's studying to be a vet for wild animals, like in a zoo." I finished.

"Rick is right," Dr. Field said. Dr. Webb walked out of the tent just then. He looked up and told her, "It's Jezebel's baby."

"I should have known!" she said. "Come child, I'm taking you home. I couldn't raise anyone near the *banda*s on the wireless."

"Aren't you going to do anything?" I asked, hurrying after her to the Range Rover. She didn't even turn around.

"Why don't you ask her to come out with us tomorrow?" Dr. Field called after her.

As soon as the car door shut, Dr. Webb started talking. "First of all, I don't believe I know your name, child."

"Anika Scott," I said. I wished she wouldn't call me *child.*

"Well, Anika Scott," she said, "I am here to study the elephants. Pure animal research requires that the researcher not interfere. If we do anything to the elephants, we change what we're studying. Do you see?"

"But, the baby!" I blurted. "It hurts him."

"Yes, it's difficult to watch," she said. "But elephants aren't tame cattle. One can't just call in the vet."

"Rick's going to be a wild animal vet," I cut in. "People do help wild animals."

She sighed. "Have you any idea what would be involved in trying to treat that baby?" She sounded angry. "Do you think his mother would let us touch him? We'd have to tranquilize her. The other family members might interfere as well. It would be dangerous for the elephants and for us."

"Oh," I said, hanging my head. "I didn't think of that."

"Didn't think! Didn't think!" she muttered furiously. "That's the trouble with people. Meddling with animals they know nothing about. Ignorant do-gooders are a menace!"

She looked over at me. I slid down in the seat and turned my head away from her.

"There is some hope that the baby will develop a false joint," she said. Her voice sounded gentler. "He seems brighter than last week. Perhaps he'll manage well enough."

I sat staring at my feet. Daddy was right. The scientists already knew all about the baby elephant. All I'd done was make myself look stupid. Now I was getting hauled back like a lost three-year-old. Besides that, I would be in big trouble. I cringed. Getting yelled at in front of Rick would be totally embarrassing.

"Which *banda* is yours?" Dr. Webb asked. She turned onto the road that ran behind the thatched cabins.

I pointed. Sandy was out beside the porch. Dr. Webb stopped behind our cabin. Sandy stared hard, then started yelling. A second later Mom was running toward the Range Rover. Dad was coming behind her. Dr. Webb yanked the parking brake on, got out, and headed toward them.

Slowly I climbed out. My thong fell off. I bent down and reached for it in the grey dust. I wasn't in a hurry to face anybody. I stood up on one foot, holding my thong, and looked uneasily at the others. Dr. Webb was talking fast, but I couldn't hear what she was saying. Rick strolled out of the house and came over to the group.

I looked up from putting my thong on. Dr. Webb was striding back toward the Range Rover.

"Thank you so much for bringing her back," Mom called after her.

Tires crunched in the gravel. I was left there, standing alone, facing my family. It was as bad as I thought.

Even worse maybe. Mom's voice sounded high and edgy. She kept telling me never to leave like that again. Daddy went on and on about how I shouldn't be so self-centered. He said that I should have thought about how other people would feel.

I shuffled my feet in the dust, trying not to cry.

"Don't you realize how badly you frightened your mother?" Daddy demanded.

"I was just trying to help the baby elephant!" I blurted desperately. "I meant to leave you a note." I spun away from them and ran for my room. Flopping onto my belly on the bed, I burst into tears. Everything was horrible. The baby elephant's leg still hurt. Dr. Webb and Dr. Field thought I was a babyish idiot. Rick thought Christians were jerks. My whole family was mad at me. Besides all that, the Geislers were trying to get us kicked out of the mission.

A few minutes later Mom came into the room. She sat on the edge of my bed. I held my breath, trying to quit crying. Her hand stroked my back gently.

"This isn't an easy time for any of us," she said. Her hands rubbed my back between my shoulder blades. Gradually I relaxed.

"Mom, I'm sorry," I said. "I wasn't thinking about you guys when I left. Later, I knew it was dumb. I mean, I almost started to come back twice."

"I know it's not easy," she said. "One of the jobs of growing up is learning to think. You're twelve. You should be thinking about the consequences your actions will have on others."

We stayed there quietly for a bit, then I asked, "Can the Geislers really get us kicked out of the mission?"

"I don't know," Mom said, and she paused. After a bit she added, "I don't really think so. The mission already knows that I had an illegitimate child as a teenager. Still . . . having him actually on the scene is diff—"

"They can't!" I interrupted, sitting bolt upright.

Mom just raised one eyebrow. "Can't? I don't know about that. I'm more worried about Rick's reaction to this. I'm praying that his anger about this won't blind him to God's love. We've got to be very careful not to make this into a fight. Dad and I think it's time to turn the other cheek and leave the outcome up to God. Even if Rick is leav—"

"Rick was already angry at Christians anyway," I interrupted. "He thinks it's Christians that are wrecking the earth. So it doesn't matter. We shouldn't just sit here and let the Geislers get us kicked out!" My voice came out high and squeaky.

"I think you need to settle down," Mom said in a no-nonsense voice. "Remember what we talked about in the car? Rick will decide what to think about Christians by how we treat each other. Do you honestly think we should begin a fight with the Geislers at this point?"

"But they're fighting with us!" I blurted. "They already wrecked everything!"

Mom shook her head, "No, I don't think so. They think that Rick's presence could do a lot of damage here. Your father and I don't agree. We think that *if* we can show how God forgives and heals—"

"So if you don't agree, go tell the field counsel!" I said, jumping in. "If they only hear what the Geislers say, that's not fair!"

"That's enough!" Mom said. "Galatians 5:14 and 15 says, 'The whole law is made complete in this one command: "Love your neighbor as you love yourself." If you go on hurting each other and tearing each other apart, be careful! You will completely destroy each other.' Is that what you want? Think about it."

She stood up and looked at me fiercely. "I want you out front, ready for lunch, in fifteen minutes, and I expect you to be in a civil frame of mind."

That verse made me think. I really hadn't been paying attention to anybody but me. I bit my lip. The whole family had been sitting around doing nothing all morning because of me.

After a bit I shut my eyes and prayed, "Please help all this to turn out OK. Sorry I went without thinking about anybody else. Please help that little elephant to be OK. Help his leg to get better. Help me not to be so mad about this thing about the Geislers. I'm so confused. Like, Rick seems OK without you, and he thinks people who belong to you do rotten things. . . . I don't get it."

I told God about the whole mess, and that made me feel better. I sighed. God was still himself even if I didn't understand.

When I came out for lunch, I said sorry for wrecking everyone's morning. That made me feel better inside too, even though it was embarrassing.

"That's OK, Sis," Rick said.

There was a long silence. Sandy was watching Rick in a funny way. I thought somebody would ask what happened to me that morning. Nobody did.

"Um . . . they couldn't help the baby. You were right, Mom," I finally said.

Mom nodded. There was another long silence. What was wrong with everybody? I was almost glad when it was time for dishes. I thought Sandy would make a fuss like she usually does. She didn't. She picked up some dishes and hurried out. I followed her.

As soon as we were out of sight of the grown-ups, she grabbed me.

"You know what happened while you were gone?" she whispered. "Rick really yelled at Mom. He's against her being a Christian. He said for her to stop fooling herself and all kinds of other things. Anyway, he said that Christianity is bad. He said he was leaving."

"Rick said he is leaving?!" I squeaked, staring at her with my mouth open.

"Shhhh!" she said. "He'll hear you."

"Rick is leaving? For sure?" I asked again.

She nodded. "I don't even care!" she whispered furiously. "Like, at first I thought it would be neat having a big brother. Not any more!"

"When is he leaving?" I asked.

"Right after lunch," she said. "That's why nobody was talking."

Chapter
Seven

~~~~~~~~~~~~~~~~~

I frowned at the cup I was washing. Why hadn't Mom told me Rick was leaving? Then I remembered. I had interrupted her when she started saying something about Rick. I bit my lip. God wasn't answering our prayers at all. It wasn't fair!

I must have been staring into space, because Sandy said, "Come on, work! You're not the only one in this family. You think you're so great running off to save baby elephants. Last night you wouldn't even answer when I called you. I know you weren't asleep. I wanted to talk about Rick and the Geislers and stuff. But you wouldn't even answer. Well, you're not so great."

My mouth fell open. That wasn't how it seemed to me at all.

"Uh, sorry," I said finally.

Sandy nodded but didn't answer. I wondered if she was trying not to cry. I couldn't think of anything to say to her.

"Anika," Daddy called, "when you're done there come on out. There's something I want to tell you."

I wrung out the dishcloth and came slowly out onto the porch. My eyes squinted against the bright outdoors sun.

"I decided I'd better tell you even if it can't happen," he said. "Dr. Webb invited you to go out with her and Dr. Field tomorrow. She invited Rick too. Apparently you told them he was training to be an exotic animal vet. We told her you won't be able to do it since we'll be leaving to see Rick off at the airport. Maybe you could write her a nice letter and visit with her another time. It would be a good chance to learn something about the animals you're so interested in."

"Oh," I said. I held my feelings down. It was no use getting upset. Everything was already too horrible.

"Hey!" Rick exclaimed. "I didn't hear about this. Who did you say that woman was?"

"Dr. Webb," Daddy said. "Dr. Margaret Webb. That's right—you didn't come out until just before she left. She's been studying the elephants in Amboseli—"

"I didn't know that woman was Margaret Webb," Rick cut in. "Margaret Webb is famous. Her work with elephants is awesome!" He looked sharply at Daddy and asked, "I have an invite to spend a day with her? That's a once-in-a-lifetime chance! I'd stay for that! Is the offer still open?"

"We can certainly find out!" Mom said. She sounded

happier than she had all morning. "You and Kevin could go over to Amboseli Lodge and radio her. See if Anika and you would still be welcome."

I might actually get to go! My stomach felt odd. I couldn't hold still. "Let it happen," I whispered, shifting from one foot to the other. "Please let it work."

As soon as Rick and Daddy were gone Sandy blurted, "That's no fair! How come Anika gets to do everything?"

"Maybe I can ask if she can come too," I said to Mom. I felt sorry for Sandy. She already felt bad. Now she had to get left out.

"I don't think Dr. Webb is the kind of person we can ask to take another child," Mom said. I sighed with relief. She went on, "If it does work out, you'll have to act very grown-up, Anika. Make sure you don't ask too many questions. I have the feeling Dr. Webb doesn't have much patience with foolishness."

"I won't," I said. "Mom, I do know *some* things—"

"It's not fair!" Sandy exclaimed stubbornly.

"Maybe you and Daddy and I can do something special together," Mom said. "The main thing is that this gives us all a little time. This could help Rick to feel better. I don't want him to leave while he is angry and rejecting us. Anika, you'll be a witness for God and for our family. Daddy and I will be praying for you."

I swallowed hard. How could I be a good witness for

God? I mean, I didn't feel that sure of things myself. Well, sometimes I did, like when I could feel God loving me. Other times it was really confusing.

Rick and Daddy found out that we could still go. That night before I went to sleep I prayed hard. I pulled my sleeping bag over my head so Sandy wouldn't hear.

"Dear God," I whispered softly. I took a breath of stuffy air and kept on, "I'm really confused. I did something bad when I left without permission to look for Dr. Field. Mom said maybe you're going to make something good out of my mistake. Like that verse, Romans 8:28 or whatever. She said maybe getting to go with Dr. Webb can help Rick. She said I have to be your witness there. I'm scared. Please help me. Especially help me make Rick not mad at you. Let him see you really care about how people treat creation. And let him quit being mad at Mom because we're missionaries."

I sighed and felt better. Then I thought of some other things I should pray about. Before I was done, I fell asleep.

The next morning Rick called softly through our door. "Wake up, Sis. Hey! Anika!"

I sat bolt upright. Rick chuckled, then said, "Come on, we'd better not keep them waiting."

He left. It was still pitch dark outside. I shivered with excitement as I reached for my clothes. I was brushing my hair when Sandy said, "Anika?" She sounded sleepy. I looked over at her underneath her mosquito net. She propped herself up on her elbow and said, "I'm going to pray for you too, OK?"

"Thanks!" I said. "Sorry I was such a jerk yesterday."

She nodded and said, "Yeah, me too. Remember you're supposed to wear shoes, not thongs."

I rolled my eyes. She always had to be right. But I did put my runners on. It turned out it was a good thing I did, too.

Outside I could still see the stars. Kilimanjaro was a dark shadow with a silver top. Rick was waiting for me with a flashlight. We walked out toward the road. Something dove through the flashlight beam that looked like a black handkerchief blowing in the wind. I jumped. Rick laughed softly. "Just a bat after a moth."

The night was full of live, silent air. Little bugs made dizzy spirals in the light of the flashlight. The bat dodged in and out after another bug. Rick's light made the rest of the night seem even darker. Something small moved on the edge of the road ahead of us. Rick swung the light. Bright green eyes blazed at us as the light caught them. There was a dim flash of patterned fur, and it was gone.

"What was that?" Rick asked softly.

"Civet cat," I said. Civet cats aren't dangerous.

They're house cat–sized with long bushy tails and pointed faces. Still, I was glad Rick was with me in the night. I wanted to tell him I was glad he was coming with me, but I couldn't find the words.

We got to the road and stood waiting. After a minute Rick turned off the flashlight, and the night opened around us. The muscle above my knee quivered as I shivered with excitement.

"Ooooo-Op! Ooooo-Op!" Hyenas were calling not too far off.

Time stretched out. *Dr. Webb must have forgotten,* I thought, biting the inside of my cheek. I looked uneasily up at Rick. He seemed like a tall stranger in the dark. Was he worried too?

The noise of an engine made me look up. Headlights were coming, far off. They bobbed up and down on the rough road. Finally the Range Rover pulled up in front of us.

After the open African night, the Range Rover felt stuffy. I looked around while Dr. Webb introduced everybody. There was a big piece of equipment in the back that hadn't been there the day before. It looked like a cross between a tape deck and a shortwave radio.

Dr. Field turned around from where he was in the front seat and said, "I hear you're going to be a wild animal vet, Rick."

"That's right," Rick said. "For me it's a way I can serve the whole of life. I don't want to see the animals as just machines. Science, because of its contamination with Christianity, often makes that mistake."

Dr. Webb gave Rick an odd look, but Rick didn't notice. He kept right on talking like he was making a speech.

"As I see it, Christian thought sees animals as money-making machines, machines that are made out of flesh. It's dominic. I mean, they figure their God told them to rule the earth."

He paused. I wanted to interrupt. I wanted to say Rick didn't understand. I wanted to so much that the words choked my throat. Still I was scared. I felt like Dr. Webb already thought I was an idiot.

Rick paused, then said, "Uh . . . I guess I don't need to convince you. Um . . . thanks again for inviting us. It's going to be great to see the elephants as a part of the whole fabric of life. For me it's a very spiritual thing, to be a part of nature, one with all that is."

I was glad when Dr. Field changed the subject.

"I don't know how much you've read, Rick," he said. "Did you know that elephants are a big part of making the grasslands?"

They started a complicated discussion about how elephants tore down trees to make grassland. That way the elephants made a place where the grazing animals could live.

What Rick had said about Christianity still bothered me. It also bothered me that I hadn't said anything. Last night I had prayed about being a good witness for God. Now I was too scared to talk. I frowned. What Rick said just wasn't true! If people treated animals like machines it was their own greedy fault, not God's!

I stared out the window. My reflection looked back at me. I could see almost nothing in the dark. We slowed down suddenly. The headlights shone on donkeylike ears and a low, humped, pale back.

"What was that?" Rick asked.

"An earth pig, aardvark," Dr. Webb said. She carefully drove around the huge hole it had dug in the track. "Unique creatures, they dig up and eat termite colonies. I do wish they'd leave the ones under the road alone. Aardvarks account for more broken axles than any other animal in Africa."

Just seeing an aardvark made me smile. If God cared enough to make odd animals like aardvarks and giraffes, he obviously liked them. He couldn't want people to treat them like machines. I frowned. Why did God let us do such rotten stuff?

"Do you think we'll find the elephant that's in heat?"

Dr. Field asked. "You said her name is Glennis, didn't you?"

"Hopefully, if she hasn't moved too far," Dr. Webb answered. "How long will it take you to get what you want?"

"If conditions are good, and she's still singing, it shouldn't take long," he answered.

Singing? I thought. *Elephants don't sing.* I wanted to ask what he meant, but I remembered what Mom had said about asking questions. I glanced over at Rick. He didn't look confused.

"They use subsonics to keep in touch, don't they?" he asked.

I frowned. What on earth were subsonics? It sounded like a new kind of submarine.

"Yes, they do use subsonics," Dr. Webb said. "The herds are matriarchal. That means they are led by females. Young elephants stay with their mother and their mother's relatives. The adult bulls stay by themselves."

"The women are more interesting to me anyway," Dr. Field said, grinning. "They talk more, like another species I could name."

Sunshine was painting the tops of the trees gold when we found Glennis. Dr. Webb turned off the engine. It was neat to be with the scientists. They were

allowed to go off the road. We were really close to the
elephants. Glennis was near a clump of thornbushes.
She looked like she was thinking, or like she had a
tummy ache. There was mud on her back. A bigger bull
elephant was near her. He had a big, dark streak of goo
running down his face.

Dr. Field had set up a mike on a stand beside the
Range Rover. Now he and Rick were back inside, looking at some dials on the recorder thing.

"Is that it?" Rick asked.

Dr. Field nodded and turned dials. I looked over. All I
could see was a bright green line on a little screen. Suddenly the line blurred and got thicker. It made a whole
lot of vibrations and then went straight again.

"There it is again! This is perfect, Margaret!" Dr. Field
said softly. "She's singing beautifully. Come on, girl . . .
Give us some more nice sonograms."

I stared at him. They were all crazy. The elephants
were perfectly quiet. Anybody knew elephants didn't
sing!

"Good girl! Beautiful!" Dr. Field said, hunched over
the recorder. "Did you feel it? Did you feel it?" he asked,
suddenly spinning toward me. "Children are supposed
to be more sensitive."

"Feel what?" I asked, moving away from him.

He threw back his head and laughed. "I'm not a dangerous lunatic. Elephants call to each other in voices lower than we can hear. When a female is in heat she sings so the best bull will come and find her. Sorry I didn't explain earlier. Now did you hear or feel anything?"

"No . . . ," I said doubtfully.

"Hssst!" Dr. Webb said suddenly.

We looked out and saw a big bull elephant coming fast. The bull by Glennis spun around. My breath caught in my throat. I looked from one bull to the other. They were going to fight. The bulls kicked up dust. They shook their big heads at each other. The newcomer was bigger than the bull that had been with Glennis. He looked huge and dangerous through the dust, like a storm god.

"It's Kamau," Dr. Webb said softly. "He shouldn't have any trouble chasing Phineas off."

If Phineas was the name of the bull that had been with Glennis, he didn't agree with Dr. Webb. He came at Kamau with a rush. The huge animals locked trunks and started shoving. Kamau loomed over Phineas. Phineas shuffled frantically backward, trying to dig in his feet.

A second later Phineas whirled and ran away. Kamau lunged after him for a few steps. Then he spun around and faced our Range Rover.

"Here comes trouble," Dr. Webb said softly. She turned the key to start the engine. The engine didn't start.

Chapter Eight

~~~~~

Kamau didn't even pause to shake his head at us. He charged. His ears were pinned back. His trunk was curled out of the way. The big bull elephant meant business. He loomed huger and huger. All I could see out my window was elephant. I scrambled away from the window. My knee whacked the top of the seat, and I tumbled into the back of the Range Rover.

The engine of the Range Rover finally started. Dr. Webb slammed it into gear. We got out of there when Kamau was only about two inches away. That's how it felt to me, anyway. He chased us for a bit, then stopped.

Dr. Webb drove for a little ways. Then she turned around and stopped. She pulled out her binoculars and looked back toward the elephants.

"There's a spiritual experience for you, Rick," said Dr. Field. He burst out laughing.

Rick laughed too, but his laugh sounded kind of shaky. He looked over to where I had been and said, "Hey! Where's Anika?"

"Um, right here," I said, trying to sound cool. I climbed back over the seat. "I thought he was going to come right through my window."

This time everybody cracked up, even me. It was great to be safe.

"What was wrong with him, anyway?" I asked.

"He was in musth," Dr. Webb said. "Did you see the discharge on the side of his face?" I nodded, and she went on. "Also he'd just won a fight. Understandably, he wanted Glennis to himself."

"What's mush, or whatever she said?" I asked Rick softly.

Dr. Field heard me and chuckled. "Watch out for bulls in musth, Anika," he said. "They'll turn you into mush."

I laughed. Dr. Field had a goofy, happy laugh.

"Musth is a period of heightened aggression in bull elephants," Dr. Webb said in her strong English accent. "When a female is in heat the strongest bull in musth who hears her sing almost always mates her. I was rather expecting Kamau to turn up."

"Speaking of singing, why don't we take a look at what we've got here," Dr. Field said.

He and Rick got busy with the recorder. Dr. Webb started writing things down in a notebook. I was staring out the window, half watching some Tommies. The car was suddenly full of sound. It was almost like whale song.

I jumped and spun around. "Awesome!" Rick said. "So that's what she sounded like."

"Only lower," Dr. Field said, chuckling. "Here, I'll speed up another call into a range that we can hear." He bent over the machine again.

"Dr. Field," I said, "um . . . you asked me if I felt anything when we were back there with the elephants. What was I supposed to feel?"

"A deep vibration," he said, looking up at me with friendly brown eyes. "That's how the low calls were discovered. Katherine Payne noticed throbbing vibration when she was near some elephants in a zoo."

"Would it jiggle your tummy?" I asked. "I didn't feel it here. It was when we were by the baby that was hurt. My insides kind of jiggled. Was that the elephant talking?"

"Very likely," he said. "Was the baby upset?"

"Well, it was getting left behind," I said uncertainly, then blurted, "It looked so tired. I wanted to help it so much!" I spun on Rick. "I don't care what you think!" I practically yelled. "God doesn't want people to treat his animals like things! The Bible says that we're supposed to take care of creation for him. They're not for us, they're for him!"

There was a small silence. My face felt hot. Dr. Webb said, "Good for you, Anika Scott. I quite agree. The creation account clearly states that God made the earth and her creatures. He found them good in themselves. Then he put them into our hands to tend and keep. I'm attempting to do so. I feel certain that God will judge us for how we've kept his creation."

I stared at Dr. Webb, open-mouthed. "Are you a Christian?" I blurted.

"I'm not sure I would mean the same thing by that as you do," she said. "But by the grace of God, yes, I am."

I glanced at Rick and Dr. Field. Both of them were looking nervous. After a second Dr. Field said, "Could we get out of the stratosphere and back to subsonics?"

"Oh," I said, "I get it. Subsonics is elephant talk."

He laughed, "Yes, *sub* means 'under,' and *sonic* means 'sound.' It's lower than the sounds we can hear. Those low kinds of sounds are called *subsonic,* or 'under sound.'"

He said the rumbles I'd felt by the baby elephant were probably made by the other elephants answering the baby's distress call. I noticed that Rick was looking out the window and frowning. I bit my lip. Was he mad about what I said to him? Was he mad at Dr. Webb now too? I saw his expression change. Now he was staring hard at something outside.

I sat up straight to see what he was looking at. Something had startled the Tommies. The little gazelles were all staring in the same direction. I looked where they were looking. There was a Masai running. His red blanket flew out behind him. He was going past us quite far away. Suddenly he stopped. He shielded his eyes for a better look. Then he ran toward us.

"Do you think we could go and get back in range for more recording?" Dr. Field asked.

"No, wait!" I blurted. "There's a man."

A few seconds later the Masai ran up and stopped by Dr. Webb's window. I could see he was really just a boy. He didn't have his hair in the Egyptian-looking braids of a *moran* yet.

"*Soba,*" he said, raising one hand in greeting. His copper skin glistened with sweat, but he wasn't even breathing hard. He said something fast in Masai and pointed back the way he had come. Dr. Webb answered him in the same language. He nodded. Then with a small skip, he broke into a run again.

Dr. Webb reached for the mike from the two-way radio. Then she paused and yelled something after the Masai. It sounded like a question. He yelled one word back. She flipped the radio on, twisted a dial, and held down the button on the mike.

"Park headquarters, come in, please. This is Margaret

Webb. Do you read me?" Loud static filled the air. She tried again, then put down the mike and started the Range Rover.

"Hey!" Dr. Field protested. He grabbed to catch his recording equipment. "What's going on?"

"Poachers!" she said through gritted teeth. "Somali poachers. The Masai boy saw their camp when he was on the way out to find his brother. He snuck away and ran for help. When he recognized my vehicle he came to me. I told him I would warn the antipoaching units. Now he's going to get help to keep people and cattle out of the way of trouble."

Dr. Webb was driving fast. We came to the road through the swamp. Dr. Webb didn't go toward the park headquarters. She turned left and headed for Lookout Hill. Lookout Hill has a place to park partway up. I'd been there lots of times. You're allowed to walk to the top. There's a kind of little porch that overlooks the swamp.

Dr. Webb took the Range Rover up the hill at a furious pace. Almost before we stopped she was on the radio again. This time she got through.

"Yes, that's right. Somali poachers," she said. "No . . . No . . . by reliable report. Send someone out to Lookout Hill immediately. Get onto the antipoaching unit . . . Yes . . . Yes!" She put down the microphone with a jerk and twisted to face us.

"Out! I want all of you out!" she said. "This is no longer a day for casual visitors. You can get a ride back from here in one of these vehicles." She waved toward the minivans that were in the parking place.

"You can hardly call me a casual visitor!" Dr. Field said. His brown eyes didn't look so friendly now.

"Neither do I want to be responsible for taking you into danger," she answered. "Somali poachers carry AK47s, Russian machine guns left from the war in Somalia. In fact, they're often soldiers who've deserted from the Somali army. Now will you get out and let me go? If I'm with the elephant herd there, the poachers won't be as likely to kill any elephants."

I looked at Rick. He was looking at me with a frown on his face. I could guess what he was thinking. He wished I wasn't there so he could go along.

"I want to come too!" I blurted. My heart was hammering madly. "It's no good just talking about taking care of animals. I want to help!"

"I will *not* take a child!" Dr. Webb said, turning to glare at Rick. "Take your sister, or half sister, or whatever the child is, and get out." She spun to face Dr. Field, "If you come, it's your own responsibility."

Rick and I climbed out. The Range Rover started downhill. Then the tires skidded. Dr. Webb had stopped. The Range Rover shot backwards up the hill toward us again.

Dr. Webb leaned out the window and yelled, "Isak is the officer of the antipoaching unit in Amboseli. I told him that there'd be instructions waiting here. Tell him that we are—" She pointed. "See that light area over there? That's Amboseli Lake. Now the Masai boy said that the poaching camp is back in the bush toward the Tanzania border from the . . . Bother! I'll just write it down. That way it's sure not to get muddled."

She dug furiously through the glove compartment, looking for a pen. A few seconds later she handed Rick a piece of paper.

"Mind that you give that to Isak!" she said. Gravel and dust spun from under the tires as they took off downhill.

Rick and I were standing alone on the rocky ground of the parking area. I sighed and shifted my feet in the gravel. Being a kid was rotten sometimes. I looked uneasily at Rick. If I hadn't been along he would proba-bly have gotten to go.

Rick was staring at the paper Dr. Webb had given him. He looked up at me with intent blue eyes. "You want to get into the action as bad as I do, don't you?"

I swallowed hard, then slowly nodded. I wanted to see, but . . . people could easily get killed. Daddy had said the antipoaching units are allowed to shoot armed poachers.

"OK," Rick said, nodding. "It might work . . . if you can read this note."

"How would that make any difference?" I asked, shrugging. "They don't need me to read them a note."

"Take a look at the note for me anyway. Can you read it?" he asked. The paper looked small in his big hands. He handed it to me. I looked at it, then nodded.

"Read it carefully," he said.

I shrugged and read it through twice. It was in Swahili. It gave directions by saying things like, "Go to the big tree on the west side of Amboseli lake, the one where the leopard was found dead. If you go straight south from there you'll find an old *manyatta* site—" There were two words I wasn't sure of. I read them over a couple of times whispering them to myself. I couldn't remember what they meant.

"Tell me what it says," Rick demanded.

"You'll never get Daddy to drive out there," I said.

"Tell me!" he insisted.

I shrugged and began to tell him, holding the paper out to show him the words. He came up close beside me to see better. His long eyelashes looked dusty. I told him I didn't know two of the words. He wanted me to memorize the whole thing, especially how to say and spell the two words.

I frowned and backed away from him. "Why? Why do you want to know this stuff?" I demanded nervously.

"Come on, Sis," he said. "Do it for me, OK?"

He had such a neat smile. Besides, we were supposed to think of others first. I shrugged and smiled. "I think you're crazy, but OK, I'll do it."

I was glad the note wasn't too long. While I was memorizing it, he kept looking along the road that came up to Lookout Hill. The people who were in the vans came down from the top. I started toward them.

Rick grabbed my arm and held me back. "We've got to wait for the antipoaching unit, remember?"

I nodded. Still, it felt funny to watch the vans drive off. Now we were out in the middle of Amboseli without any car.

"Who did Margaret Webb say we were supposed to give the note to?" Rick asked. "Esau?"

"No, Isak," I answered. It's no wonder Rick got mixed up. The way *Isak* sounded was "Eesok."

Rick said the name to himself. He made me say the whole note back to him twice. He held the note and checked me. Luckily, Swahili is spelled the same way it sounds. He made me tell him what I thought the note said in English. He repeated it back to me.

"What are you going to do?" I asked as soon as he was done. "Steal our car and try to—"

"Hsst!" he said, pointing toward the road. "Does that look like what we've been waiting for?"

A Land Rover was coming fast. I could see that it was crammed with men. Rick suddenly snatched the note out of my hand. He pulled a lighter out of his pocket and set the note on fire.

"Hey!" I yelled, grabbing for the paper. I jerked my hand back from the flame. "Don't burn it!"

"Do you want to go along, or not?" he demanded.

"Well, I guess," I said. "But—"

"So now we have to," he said. He dropped the note onto the ground so it could finish burning. He was pushing dust over the ashes with his foot when the Land Rover stopped. My mouth felt dry, like I was part lizard. I couldn't seem to get enough air.

The man driving the Land Rover was very black. His green bush hat shaded his eyes. He leaned out into the sunlight looking at us.

"Jambo," he said in a deep voice. *"Wapi memsabu Webb?"*

I swallowed with a dry throat. He had asked where Dr. Webb was in Swahili. I answered in the same language, wishing that Rick could talk instead. "She has gone to guard the elephants," I said. "She has left instructions—"

"Is he Isak?" Rick interrupted.

I glared at him. Why did he burn the note and get me into this anyway? The man driving the Land Rover said in Swahili, "I am Isak Abdul."

I turned away from Rick and explained that we had a message. I said that I had been made to memorize it. That was true, even if it wasn't the whole truth. Isak looked at me kind of funny when I said that. I never thought of tattling on Rick. If there's one thing you learn at boarding school, it's never to tattle. Besides, it wouldn't have done any good. I'd still have to tell them the message.

I finished telling him the message. Isak picked up a mike and started talking on the radio very fast.

"What's going on?" Rick asked.

"I think he's talking to a helicopter . . . ," I said uncertainly.

"Did you give him the message straight?"

I frowned and nodded without looking at Rick. Suddenly Isak motioned for both of us to get into the Land Rover. One of the men in the front climbed into the back. We crammed into the front seat. My heart pounded in my ears. Rick's plan had worked.

Chapter
Nine

~~~~~~~~~~~~~~~~~~~~~~~~

Please, God, I prayed silently as we bumped down the hill. My mouth felt dry as sawdust. *I didn't mean to do anything wrong. I didn't know Rick was going to burn the note. Just keep us safe.*

I was practically sitting on Rick's lap. He was jammed up against the door. The man between me and the driver had a belt with bullets in it. The butt of his rifle was sticking into my ribs. I looked at him nervously. The Land Rover smelled of sweat.

Isak yelled over the noise in the Land Rover, "I have told the antipoaching helicopter. You will go with them to point the spot. We will wait for them by the lake. He is already coming from Tsavo."

"But I don't know this place," I said desperately. "I only know Dr. Webb's directions."

He jerked his head to point at the man sitting between us. "Loragoi will go with you. He knows the land. Already he says he knows the place Dr. Webb speaks of."

"What?" Rick asked in my ear. He didn't know what was going on because it was all in Swahili.

"He said I have to go in the helicopter with one of the *askari*s," I said. I was still mad at Rick, but I was scared that they'd separate us.

"*Askari*s?" Rick asked.

I shook my head. "It means 'guards' or 'soldiers' or whatever, like these men," I said.

One of the men in the backseat yelled something. The Land Rover skidded to a halt. All the *askari*s piled out. Rick and I followed.

"There!" one of the men said in Swahili, pointing up.

The black speck was getting bigger. Isak switched off the Land Rover engine. Immediately we could hear the steady *whup, whup, whup* of a helicopter. Another man grabbed a red cloth out of the back of the Land Rover and started waving it.

"Hey!" Rick blurted, looking up at the helicopter. "That's a Bell Huey gunship!"

I bit my lip and watched. The helicopter got bigger and bigger and louder and louder. The doors in the side were open. There was a big machine gun on the outside, below the doors. A blast of wind hit us as the helicopter landed.

"Come!" Loragoi yelled in my ear over the helicopter noise. His hand felt callused when he grabbed my arm.

Pulling me after him, he started running toward the helicopter. Noise, dust, gravel, and wind beat at me. Loragoi ran crouched down. The huge rotor blades were slashing through the air just above me.

I twisted away from Loragoi and looked for Rick. He was right behind me. We climbed into the open door of the helicopter. Rick gave me a thumbs-up signal. He had a big grin on his face. My heart gave a thudding leap. For a second I grinned too. *Talk about exciting!* I thought, as the helicopter gave a jerk and went up. Then my smile faded. I stared at the rifles the men were carrying.

It got even noisier. Rick was looking into the cockpit, grinning like an idiot. There were at least ten African men in the helicopter dressed in the same uniform as Loragoi. One of them yelled something at Loragoi. Loragoi followed him toward the cockpit.

I looked back out the door. There was just air between me and the ground. I could see the flat, grey pan of Amboseli Lake. At first I couldn't see the Land Rover. Then, there it was, looking like a micromachine. It was tearing along a road after us, trailing a plume of dust behind it. A herd of giraffes was running away from the noise of the helicopter. It looked odd from straight up.

Somebody thumped me on the shoulder. My stomach

jerked. I whirled around. One of the men from the helicopter motioned for me to follow him. We went forward on the vibrating metal floor. Rick yelled something at me that I couldn't hear. He was still grinning. I ended up standing behind the pilot. One of the flight crew pulled a helmet off his head and put it on me. It fell down over my eyes. I shoved it up so I could see. Suddenly I realized I could hear the men talking. The helmet had earphones in it.

"Jambo mtoto," somebody said. That means, "Hello, child." I looked around wildly to see who was talking. The man who had put the helmet on me pulled something down from the top of my helmet. It ended up in front of my mouth. It was a tiny microphone. These helmets were like the ones fighter pilots wear in the movies.

Again a man's voice greeted me. This time I saw it was the copilot. *"Jambo,"* I answered, trying to make my voice sound steady and grown-up.

"Loragoi has said you have the instructions. Please repeat them," the voice said in my ear.

I swallowed and repeated the instructions, trying to get them exactly right.

"Good. Thank you, child," the voice said. The man took the helmet back. Just before he pulled it off my head I heard Loragoi talking. I could see him pointing. I moved over to see what he was pointing at and ended up next to Rick.

Rick put his mouth right in my ear and yelled, "I think they've found the poachers' camp. You're doing OK, Sis."

I shook my head and pointed at what I'd seen out the window. It was a dead elephant. It looked flat, like it had been printed on the dusty ground. Around it were the black shapes of vultures.

We went past the dead elephant. A few minutes later we slowed down until we were hovering. Loragoi was pointing and motioning that we should go down. Another man seemed to be arguing with him.

Two men pulled black visors over their faces. They swung the machine guns around in front of the doors. Rick and I were shoved back into a corner. My mouth tasted like old metal. They were getting ready to shoot!

The helicopter went down so low I could see trees out the window. We hovered, then moved, and hovered again. Both of the machine guns started firing. I could see the empty shells from the bullets fly through the air. We spun in a circle.

One of the men by the door shook his head. An *askari* near me yelled, "They are not there."

Rick stood up. I did too. My stomach felt very weird. We went down and landed in a clear area. I could see a place where there had been a campfire. After a second I realized that some of the branches of the bushes were cut to make shelters. It was the poachers' camp.

Loragoi was out first. He ran zigzagging over the ground like a dog looking for a scent. He watched the ground as he went. His head and shoulders hunched forward. A second later another man joined him, moving in the same way.

Loragoi laid a hand on the ashes of the fire. Then he called back, "They are gone since this morning."

"Have they taken the ivory?" the officer called. "Will they return?"

Both men who had got out began to circle at a trot. They were carefully looking at the ground in a wide area around the camp. They called back and forth to each other.

"It was not here, they have gone," Loragoi called.

"Perhaps they have buried it where they have killed," the other man called.

The officer nodded and said, "Let us go and see the place of the dead elephant."

Loragoi and the other tracker climbed in. The rotors thundered and we were off again. I thought we would land right beside the dead elephant. Instead we landed way over to the side.

I must have looked puzzled because Rick yelled in my ear, "They don't want vultures in the rotor blades or turbine."

The noise of the engine stopped halfway through what he said. Rick's voice suddenly stood out by itself. A horrible smell came in through the door in a thick wave. Everyone climbed out. Loragoi and another man trotted toward the dead elephant. Rick started to follow him.

"Stop!" the pilot said in English. "The trackers must look first."

I put my hand over my face because of the smell. The vultures were coming back down. Black feathers on the ends of their long wings looked like splayed fingers. One thumped down not far from us. He hopped crookedly toward the dead elephant. The pilot had stayed in the helicopter. I heard him say something to Isak on the radio.

After a few minutes Loragoi came back. "This elephant is dead five or six days," he said. "When they took the tusks, they buried them close. We have found the place. Just this morning they have come back to get the tusks. The tracks are fresh, maybe one hour."

I heard another man say that Isak's Land Rover was coming. That man was handing out automatic rifles and ammunition. The sight of them getting ready to use rifles scared me. It made me madder at Rick for burning that paper.

"What's going on?" Rick asked.

I ignored him.

"What are they saying?" Rick said again. "Come on, Sis, don't be a jerk."

"Who's the jerk?" I whispered so the *askari* wouldn't hear us arguing.

I turned my back on Rick and tried to listen. I wanted to know what the *askari*s would tell us to do. The noise of the Land Rover made me jump. It came in in a swirl of choking dust. Men climbed out with their rifles ready. All the *askari*s, even the men from the helicopter, trotted off toward the dead elephant.

Rick followed them. He motioned me to come. I shook my head. He shrugged and kept going. I stood shifting uneasily from foot to foot. I didn't know the helicopter pilot had stayed. After a second, scared to be alone, I ran after Rick.

I caught up before they got to the elephant. The vultures went away from us. They hopped across the ground, flapping their wings. Suddenly I could see the elephant. I felt hot and dizzy. My brain felt too big for my skull, and my stomach heaved. I threw up into the dust. Everybody was staring at me. The smell and the buzz of flies choked me.

I ran straight away from there. A branch tripped me. I scrambled up and stood there panting. Somebody was coming behind me. Two little black-backed jackals darted past.

I glanced back. It was Rick. Crossing my arms I turned stiffly away from him.

"Hey, I'm sorry," he said putting a big, warm hand on my shoulder. "I shouldn't have gotten you into this. My stomach doesn't feel too great either."

I stood there stiffly with my shoulders hunched. My mouth tasted horrible. I shifted my feet. *It's no use being mad at him,* I thought. *Besides, we're supposed to forgive.* I wiped at my mouth with the back of my hand and said, "It's OK."

There was a small silence. Suddenly I realized maybe this was my chance to explain things to Rick. *Please, God, help,* I thought.

Quickly, before I could chicken out, I said, "Um . . . Mom really cares about you. She cried when she told us how she had to give you up."

I took a quick look at Rick. He had gone absolutely still. I went on, "See, don't be mad because we're Christians, OK? We don't always do the right stuff, but that doesn't mean God isn't real. God does care about nature and the stuff he created. Dr. Webb even said so. Don't be mad. I mean, Mom was really sad. She said I had to be God's witness to you today."

Rick was looking at me now. He had one eyebrow up like he was thinking, *Oh, sure.*

"No, really!" I blurted. "It's confusing sometimes, but

God is real. He helps us do the right stuff. Like Mom and Daddy aren't even mad at the Geislers. God even loves you, too."

Rick turned his head away from me. He stood there staring into the distance. Suddenly his whole body tensed.

"Sis, look!" he whispered. "Do you see what I see?"

Through a gap in the bush I could see something moving. It was men, men with rifles. They were quite far away. I looked again. They didn't have uniforms on. They weren't *askari*s.

"It's the poachers!" I said in a scared squeak.

Rick grabbed me and pulled me down behind a bush. He stared at the poachers. My throat was so tight I could hardly breathe.

The poachers trotted out of sight. Rick twisted toward me. He grabbed both of my shoulders so hard it hurt. "We've got to stop them!" he whispered, giving me a little shake. "I'll tell the helicopter pilot. He talked English to me. You have to find the others and tell them."

For a second I stayed frozen. Rick ran quickly and quietly back into the bush. I whispered, "But the pilot went with the other *askari*s."

My heart thudded in my ears. I thought it was all up to me now. I ran toward the elephant carcass.

I tore into the clearing where the dead elephant was.

Vultures ran clumsily away, lunging into the air. I stopped, looking around. No one was there. The huge heap of the dead elephant blocked my view. I dashed around it. Nothing. Nothing but vultures and flies in the thick, hot sun.

"Isak! Loragoi!" I yelled. Only silence answered.

The poachers couldn't get away! They couldn't! I opened my mouth to call again. The helicopter's big rotor started. I bit my lip, wondering wildly if Rick was trying to fly it.

Suddenly I remembered Loragoi looking at tracks. I looked down. Footprints were clear in the dust around the carcass. *The askaris' tracks have to be on top,* I told myself. They would come from the helicopter. Chewing my cheek nervously I ran back around the elephant to the path from the helicopter. I found a clear set of tracks on the path and started to follow it. It wasn't as easy as I thought. Even in soft dust the tracks kept getting underneath each other.

I followed the tracks a little way away from the elephant. Then I heard running feet. I dodged toward the nearest thornbush and hid. The bush was too thick, tangled, and spiky to hide under properly. There was no more time. I froze with my back up against thorn tangle and waited. If it was poachers with rifles, I didn't have a hope.

The whole antipoaching patrol swept past running hard. I jumped up, digging thorns into my back. Twisting away from the thorns, I yelled, "Wait! I saw the poachers."

They ignored me and kept running. I looked back the way they'd come. What if more poachers were chasing them?

Chapter
Ten

I ran after the *askari*s of the antipoaching unit as hard as I could run. Even the smell of the dead elephant didn't slow me down. The helicopter was already taking off when I got there. Most of the *askari*s were in it.

Isak and some others were climbing into the Land Rover.

"Wait!" I yelled again.

The Land Rover was already starting to roll. I ran toward it and grabbed onto the back. Two *askari*s reached out to pull me in so I wouldn't fall.

"I saw the poachers," I yelled at Isak.

"The helicopter pilot has said," he said, patting the radio he had slung over his shoulder. "Your brother told him. We are following him."

We all ducked as the Land Rover tore under a low thornbush. Bits of thorn and leaves sprayed over me.

"They are there!" I yelled, pointing in the direction we'd seen the poachers.

"Were they in a vehicle?" another *askari* asked, yelling over the noise of the Land Rover.

I answered him, clutching at the side to keep my balance. A second later I heard machine guns stuttering. The helicopter was right ahead. I could see men in the door firing at something on the ground. The *askari* beside me shoved me down flat. My face was right on the gritty floor of the Land Rover. I started to get up, and he shoved me down harder. My head banged the floor.

"Stay there!" he said fiercely.

The Land Rover swerved. I banged into the side. It slowed down and thumped over something. I stuck out my hands and feet to brace myself. A man stepped on me. Then he jumped out the back. I was facing the back of the Land Rover. I looked out. The man didn't land on his feet. He rolled on the ground on purpose until he was behind a bush. The *askari*'s hand shoved me down again.

A second later another man jumped out, then another. I think we made a big circle before the Land Rover jerked to a stop. One man stayed. I lifted myself up. The others were disappearing into the bush at a crouching run. I could hear machine guns firing over the noise of the helicopter. Bullets whanged off the metal of the Land Rover. I pressed my face into the grit on the metal Land Rover floor.

Akakakaka! The *askari* standing beside the Land
Rover opened fire. I curled into a ball and covered my
ears. The only thing I could think was, *Don't let Rick
get killed. Don't let Rick get killed. He doesn't know
you yet.* Somehow I never even thought that I might
get hurt or killed.

For a few minutes the helicopter thundered, hovering right overhead. The grit on the floor hurt my cheek.
More rifle fire cracked through the air. After what
seemed like ages, I heard the helicopter land. I could
hear men's voices talking and yelling.

Even after the noise of fighting stopped, I stayed
where I was. Finally I sat up, feeling stiff and shaky. Out
the back of the Land Rover I couldn't see anything but
thornbushes in the sunshine. As I climbed out, a bottle
bird called. It seemed odd that the bird would sound
normal. I stood up in the sun on the dusty ground and
looked around.

The first thing I saw was Rick going toward the helicopter. He was half carrying an *askari.* The *askari* was
dragging one leg. I ran toward them. Rick was handing
the man up to other people in the helicopter when he
saw me.

"Sis! You're here!" he bellowed.

He let go of the man and grabbed me in a bear hug.
"I thought you got left back by the dead elephant," he

said. "I was worried about you." He looked at me. "You're all right?"

I nodded and laughed, "You, too!"

He let go of me suddenly and said, "When the shooting started I felt sick. I mean, it hit me that I really care about you. I should never have got you into this. It was a stupid thing to do."

I grinned at him and said, "It's OK. Hey, what happened to the poachers?"

"They've got them in the Bell Huey helicopter already," he said. "Two are hurt pretty bad."

"I thought they'd all be dead," I blurted. "There was so much shooting."

"They fired around the poachers a lot to get them to surrender," Rick said. "Some wouldn't quit shooting at us, and they got hurt. They're flying the hurt men out. The pilot said he'd drop you and me off with Dr. Webb on the way. The men with the Land Rover are going to try to track two poachers who got away. Just a sec. I'll be right back."

Rick dodged into the helicopter. The Land Rover pulled up beside me right then. Men started picking up stuff the poachers had dropped and loading it into the Land Rover. There were machine guns and odd bundles.

"Hey, Sis!" Rick called from the helicopter door. "The pilot says you can ride up front."

When we were getting in, I heard one of the hurt poachers groaning. It made me feel scared and sick. Afterwards I figured out that Rick probably got the pilot to let me go up front so I wouldn't notice the wounded poachers so much. I guess it kind of worked. I couldn't hear them moaning with the intercom helmet on, anyway.

The pilot showed me how the complicated joystick thing he called the "collective" worked. The collective made us go up and down. Then there was another stick between his knees called the cyclic. That made us go forward or sideways. There were rudder pedals on the floor that helped turn. With all the dials and instruments it looked very complicated. I glanced back at the hurt men and shivered.

Loragoi had come with the helicopter. He thought he knew where Dr. Webb was. He stood behind the pilot, looking out the front and giving directions.

"There!" he said, pointing. A few seconds later I saw the elephants, too. Dr. Webb's Range Rover was on the far side. I counted twenty-four elephants before we started coming down.

"Why are we coming down so far away?" I asked.

"We do not wish to frighten the elephants so much," the pilot answered. "Take off the helmet and go back to the door. You must get off quickly."

Dr. Field ran toward us. He was yelling something, but we couldn't hear him. The helicopter made too much noise. As soon as the skids touched the ground Rick and Loragoi jumped down. I followed. My head felt odd. The wind from the rotor was twisting my hair in all directions. The pilot didn't wait to see what Dr. Field wanted.

Dr. Field stopped running as soon as he realized the helicopter wasn't waiting. We stood and watched it disappear. The noise got farther and farther away.

"What were you running to tell them?" I asked Dr. Field as soon as we could hear to talk.

"The elephant herd is missing one family group," he said. "We tried to talk to you on the radio but couldn't get through. Margaret wanted to use the helicopter to look for them. They might be away from the larger group somewhere." He shook his head and said, "Instead of studying the animals, we have to fight for their existence."

I looked at Rick. Would he say something about how poaching was Christians' fault? He didn't say anything.

"Hey," Dr. Field said. "What were you two doing in the antipoaching helicopter anyway? Didn't Margaret succeed in cutting you out of the action?"

Rick grinned and shrugged.

The Range Rover came over and stopped beside us. *"Jambo,* Loragoi," Dr. Webb called, climbing out. Then in Swahili she asked Loragoi if he had seen certain elephants. She listed them by name.

Loragoi looked at his feet. He said slowly, "I have not seen Njiru, Norah, or Fupi. Joshua is dead. He is there. They had killed him five or six days ago."

Dr. Webb spun away from us and stood still. I looked at her, wondering if she was crying. Rick and Dr. Field looked confused. Neither of them knew Swahili, so they didn't know what Loragoi had said. No one moved.

She spun back suddenly and said furiously in English, "Those dirty—! He barely had any ivory at all!" She changed into Swahili. "Loragoi, were the tracks of the others near Joshua? Could we follow the elephants from there?"

Loragoi considered, then slowly said, "Perhaps it is too long a time. Maybe it is possible."

A few minutes later we were all in the Range Rover heading back to the dead elephant. Loragoi had climbed in front with Dr. Webb to show the way. Rick, Dr. Field, and I were in the back.

"So how'd you get included in this?" Dr. Field asked. He tipped his head in the direction of Dr. Webb and said with a grin, "She's not easy to thwart."

"Told them we had to give instructions. When the shooting started, it didn't seem like such a good idea after all."

"And?" Dr. Field asked.

Rick started telling about finding the empty camp, then the dead elephant. "Sis, here, was the one who spotted the poachers," he said, then grinned. "The dead elephant proved a bit much for her stomach." His smile faded. "Mine too, almost. But we got the jerks."

"Why do people poach?" I cut in. "I mean, that man that got shot, I felt really sorry for him."

Dr. Field shrugged. "For people like these Somalis, it's a way to make money. They can use the weapons and skills they got in the war there. They see no harm in shooting all the elephants they can."

"Killing for pleasure and profit," Rick said. "The best hunter is a dead hunter as far as I'm concerned."

My heart did a double thud. Uncle Paul Stewart, one of my favorite people, liked hunting.

Dr. Field cut in, "I can't agree with you there. In North America most of the money for conservation comes from hunters. Animal rights activists talk a lot, but hunters are the ones who pay to keep wild land for the animals. Groups like Ducks Unlimited buy and preserve huge tracts of wild land."

"It's self-interest," Rick said, frowning. "They only do it so they've got something to shoot."

"Uncle Paul cares about nature!" I blurted. "I bet he knows more about it than you do!"

Both Rick and Dr. Field laughed. Rick said, "Hey, easy, Sis. I wasn't trying to put down your Uncle Paul."

Dr. Webb must not have been listening. Suddenly she said, "Norah has her first baby with her. Maybe they haven't killed him."

"Maybe the other elephants didn't get shot at all," I said hopefully. Dr. Webb just looked at me out of angry eyes.

Loragoi did find the tracks of the other elephants. He trotted back and forth, staring at tracks none of the rest of us could see at all. Slowly we followed him in the Range Rover. Before we'd gone very far, he stopped and pointed. In the distance I saw the black shapes of vultures circling. Loragoi ran toward the Range Rover. A second later we were going full speed toward the vultures.

All three of the other elephants were there. They were dead. Two were almost together. The third was a couple of hundred yards away. I swallowed convulsively at the smell. "I will not puke! I will not puke!" I whispered to myself.

Loragoi said something rapidly in Swahili. He pointed at the third dead elephant. I looked and saw the top of a baby elephant's back on the far side. Dr. Webb got out and walked slowly toward the baby. She motioned us to stay away. She got quite close and stood watching for a while. When she came back, she flicked the radio on.

"Park headquarters, come in. This is Margaret Webb. Do you read me?" She had to try a couple of times. Finally, through pops and fizzes, we heard an answer.

"We've located an orphaned elephant. Dehydrated. Ask for air transport. Repeat, ask for air transport for orphaned elephant. Will bring in to main strip."

I couldn't hear the answer over the static, but Dr. Webb did. Anyway, she repeated the message again, then signed off.

She twisted in her seat to look at me. "Anika, this is one baby we may be able to help. Or, rather, take to someone who can help."

"Elanor Hales?" Dr. Field asked. He kept looking over at the baby with its dead mother. "Is she the one you're planning to take this baby to?"

"Oh! Uncle Paul told me about her," I cut in. "She's the one that lives in Nairobi Game Park, right? She raises baby elephants and rhinos so they can be wild again."

Dr. Webb nodded her head and said, "First we have to catch the baby. Then—"

"Catch an elephant! What with?" Rick interrupted.

"With our hands—gently!" She said the last word fiercely. "It's only a baby, and it's weak and frightened."

"Right," Rick said. "If I'm going to be an exotic animal vet, there couldn't be a better time to start."

She had us all make a circle around the baby elephant. Slowly, slowly we walked toward it. It stumbled closer to its dead mother. My throat was choked with excitement and fear and feeling sorry for the baby all at once. As we got closer the baby looked bigger to me. He was almost as tall as my waist. He squealed and spun to face us, then, stumbling, he ran right into Loragoi. Loragoi scrambled backwards to keep from falling. He hung onto the baby elephant. All the rest of us ran up to help. The elephant's skin felt rougher than I thought it would.

"Gently, gently," Dr. Webb said. "Easy, easy. There, little fellow . . ."

After a few seconds of struggling, the baby stood still. I could feel him trembling. Half pushing, half lifting, we walked the baby elephant over to the Range Rover.

"You three hold him," Dr. Webb said to the three men. "Anika, come help me clear out the back of the vehicle." We were getting in when she called back to the men, "Talk to him, stroke him. He's just a frightened infant."

We piled everything into the front until the front seat was just a big heap of junk. Then she opened the back, and we got back out. I wondered how we'd ever get the little elephant into the Range Rover. He looked too big to pick up.

Loragoi motioned to Rick. He and Rick locked arms under the baby's belly and lifted. Everybody else tried to help. I ended up with the baby's back leg kicking my stomach. I hung on grimly with my face against the rough, dirty skin.

I could hear things like, "Ouch!" "OK, OK, easy," "A little bit to the left, no, *my* left!" I realized the baby was going forward, away from me. He was in! Loragoi and Dr. Field had got in alongside him. Rick and I were outside. Dr. Webb shut the back and looked at us with her hands on her hips. There was no more room inside the Range Rover. I bit my lip. Would she leave us behind?

Chapter
Eleven

~~~~~~~~~~~~~~~~~~~~~~~~~~~

"There's no room inside," Dr. Webb said finally. "You'll have to ride on the front of the Range Rover."

"All right!" I yelled and ran to climb on.

"Mind you, hold tight!" she said and slammed her door.

Riding on the front of a Land Rover through the bush was one of my favorite things. Range Rovers were almost as good, only there wasn't as much to hold on to. Rick and I ducked into the middle as we scraped between two thornbushes. Then we were on the road.

I grinned into the wind, shifting to keep my balance on the bumps. A bunch of yellow-necked spur fowl flew up in front of us. We came to some ostriches close to the road. One dodged onto the road. It started to run in front of us. Its black-and-white feathers bobbed in time to its huge strides. Each stride kicked up a puff of dust.

"Africa is the best!" I yelled at Rick over the wind. He grinned and gave me a thumbs-up sign. Then he had to grab to keep his balance.

A few minutes later we stopped beside the air strip. Actually, we weren't right by the strip. Dr. Webb parked under the nearest shade trees. She turned off the engine. Silence poured in around us. I looked back through the windshield. Dr. Webb was talking on the radio. She finished and climbed into the back with the baby elephant. No one got out.

Rick and I stayed sitting on the front of the Range Rover. I could hear grasshoppers clicking as they flew from one clump of grass to another. It was the middle of the afternoon now and really hot. I stretched my neck, trying to see the baby elephant. Between Dr. Webb and Dr. Field all I could see was the top of its head.

"Do you think it will die?" I asked Rick nervously.

He looked at me and shrugged. "I don't know. Wild babies of any kind aren't easy to keep alive. This one is already pretty stressed out. It must have been without food or water since its mother was killed. Don't get your hopes up too much."

Dr. Field climbed out of the Range Rover and came around front. "Margaret figures it's going to be a while until the plane arrives," he said. "Do you want us to call on the radio for someone to come pick you up? Won't your parents be getting worried?"

"Could you leave a message for them that we're here?" I blurted.

Dr. Field grinned at me. "Don't want to be left out? I don't blame you. OK, we'll try."

He climbed back in the Range Rover.

I hugged my knees. Why did parents have to worry so much anyway, I wondered. I glanced at Rick. He was leaning back on the windshield with his eyes closed. There was a smear of dirt over the strong bones of his cheek.

"You're really lucky!" I blurted.

He raised his eyebrows without opening his eyes.

"You can just do whatever. Nobody worries about you."

He laughed and sat up. "I don't know about that. I'm going back to see if I can help with the elephant. Want to come?"

Rick asked if we couldn't try to get some fluid into the baby elephant.

"Go ahead," Dr. Webb said. "It can't hurt."

"Fluid?" I asked.

"He's probably very dehydrated," Rick said. "He could die of thirst. The best thing would be a balanced electrolyte, to replace the salts he's lost. Water is better than nothing."

He got a cup full of water from the Thermos and tried to get the baby elephant to swallow it. The baby struggled and wouldn't open its V-shaped mouth. When he forced its mouth open the water just ran out. He didn't do it again. The little elephant was getting too upset.

"Maybe he'd suck on a cloth," I said. I felt like crying.

The radio crackled and started talking. It was a plane. The plane for the baby elephant was coming already.

The engine droned louder and louder. It came down low right over us. I could see the numbers and letters underneath the wing. It went up looking small and white in the blue sky. Then it landed. The plane turned around and came taxiing toward us. The big propeller on the front was slicing through the air.

A man leapt out and ran across the grass. His bush hat flipped off, and the wind from the propeller blew his grey hair.

"Margaret!" he said, putting down a medical bag to stick out his hand. "So sorry about your elephants. Elanor Hales asked me to come get this baby as I was already in Tsavo."

A minute later they were walking the baby toward the plane. I walked alongside praying in my head, *Don't let him die. Please don't let him die.* At the plane Rick crowded in to watch the man put an intravenous needle into the baby elephant. That was to replace the fluid the baby had lost.

A few minutes later the plane disappeared into the sky. Stillness and bright sun surrounded us.

Dr. Webb said matter-of-factly, "Well, we'd better get you two home."

Partway down the road we met Mom, Daddy, and Sandy coming to pick us up.

"Thank you for letting us come," I said as we climbed out of the Range Rover. "It was awesome! I'd really like to do your kind of job."

Dr. Field laughed, "I wouldn't call today a typical day. Would you, Margaret?"

"I should hope *not,*" she said. "It's usually hours and hours of recording boring details."

"It wouldn't be boring to me!" I said.

It felt good to get into our own safe, familiar car. I suddenly realized I was filthy dirty, tired, and starving.

"Hey!" Sandy blurted before anybody had a chance to say anything, "Know what? The Geislers left a message for Daddy to call, and you know what happened when he did? The mission said Rick being here is OK!"

"All right!" I yelled.

"Wait a minute," Daddy said, "it's not that simple. We can discuss this later."

"Yes," Mom cut in. "First you have to tell us hut whappened to you."

Everybody laughed at Mom's mixed-up words. Rick and I both started talking at once. He didn't tell about how he'd burned the note so I didn't either.

I guess Daddy figured there was something wrong. He said, "Margaret Webb left and asked you to give directions to the antipoaching squad?"

Neither of us answered his question. Rick just kept on telling what happened.

But Daddy gave me a look in the rearview mirror that said he was going to want to hear more about it, later. I knew I'd have to tell what really happened.

"You actually touched a baby elephant?" Sandy blurted. She kept asking and asking everything about it. Sweat trickled down my stomach in a ticklish line. I rubbed my hand against it. My hand left a dirty smear on my shirt.

"Mom," I said, interrupting Sandy. "Can't we go some-where to get clean and eat, maybe at Amboseli Lodge? The tub at the cabin is gross. Besides, there's a pool at the lodge. I'm roasting."

There was a silence and Daddy said slowly, "You know we can't afford—"

"I'll treat," Rick cut in. "Just say I want to buy my African family a meal. Besides I feel like I could eat—"

"An elephant?" Sandy asked with a grin on her face.

"Gross!" I yelled, remembering the dead elephants I'd seen that day. "No way!"

That afternoon was the best. We ordered our food by the pool. It felt so good to stand under the shower and get clean, then dive into the cool pool. We raced and splashed and dunked each other. Daddy even played keep-away with us. Rick was a really good swimmer. The muscles on his back and shoulders shone in the sun. He did the butterfly stroke. Sandy and I tried to copy him, but we ended up in giggles. It wasn't as easy as he made it look.

Nothing ever tasted as good as the hamburger I ate. I was on my last bite when Rick said, "Hey, um, there's something I've got to say." We all looked at him. He ducked his head. Then he looked up with his dark blue eyes. "This isn't easy, but, ah, I was wrong to get mad at you yesterday." He looked at Mom. "I realize that you're a separate person with a whole separate life from me. Sorry I tried to jerk you around and make you change. You haven't done that to me."

There was a little silence. I could feel my heart beating. A huge smile was starting somewhere deep inside me.

Daddy said, "It hasn't been an easy time for any of us. I'm sorry if I wasn't as sensitive as I should have been."

"Hey man, no sweat," Rick said. "You all have been great, even my kid sisters."

"Does this mean you aren't going away?" Sandy said, grinning happily. "You're staying, right?"

Rick was shaking his head. "I've got to get back," he said.

"Could you stay a few more days?" Daddy asked. "The mission has asked us to make a public statement about what has happened in our family. We'll do that in church this Sunday. It would be good if you could stay until then."

"If you can't, don't worry," Mom said.

"If you stay we could maybe get permission to visit the baby elephant," I cut in. "Right, Daddy? I mean, we helped catch it and everything."

Rick laughed and said, "OK, but I can't stay long. My real life is still back in Oregon."

"Are the Geislers still mad at us?" I asked. "Is that why you have to do this public statement thing?"

"Anika, you know they were never mad at us," Mom said in a shame-on-you voice. "They just saw things differently. They aren't happy with the mission's ruling, but they've agreed to accept it."

"Will they stop being friends with us?" I asked. "I thought they were really nice at first." I was watching a boy with an ice-cream cone walk by.

"We'll just have to wait and see," Mom said. "It may be awkward for a while—"

"Can we have some ice cream?" Sandy asked. "Please! Please! I'm still starving!"

The next couple of days were fun. Even the hot drive back to Mumbuni wasn't bad. Everybody was friendly, relaxed, and normal. The only thing was, Rick still didn't stick around for family devotions.

I don't think I've ever been so nervous as I was that Sunday. Mom came into my room looking for something while I was getting dressed.

"How come we have to go into Nairobi?" I asked, pulling my dress straight. Suddenly I hated the peachy color of the dress I had on. I yanked at it again and repeated, "Why can't we just do it here?"

Mom sighed and said, "Anika, don't make trouble now. We've agreed to do what they said. They want us where most of the African church council can come and listen. The whole point is to tell the truth openly in public. That way no gossip can start. Also it's a chance to clearly state that we do not think sex outside marriage is acceptable. Besides, Rick is leaving in the evening, so we'd have to go into Nairobi today anyway."

I bit my lip. Mom looked white and worried. "Are you scared, too?" I asked.

She nodded. We ended up hugging each other. Then Mom prayed, "Please, God, let this be a day where everything works together to honor you. Keep us from doing anything that would hurt your work in the church, or in Rick's life, or in our family's life."

"At least we got permission to visit Elanor Hales in

the afternoon," I said. "She said the baby elephant was still alive, right?"

Mom nodded. "She said if he lives till this weekend he has a good chance. I guess you'll find out when we get there, Anika. Just remember, unfair things happen sometimes."

We drove into the parking lot by Nairobi Bethel Church. People in bright Sunday clothes were coming from all directions. I swallowed hard and glanced at Rick. He looked like he wished he could disappear.

We got out of the car. Jane Njiru and her family came over to greet us. I liked Jane because she was friendly and smiled a lot. Also she had gorgeous clothes and hairstyles. Today her hair was done in thousands of little braids.

"Welcome! Welcome," she said, shaking Rick's hand. Then she looked at Mom and Daddy and said, "We are with you all the way. We have been praying and praying for you. I know God will work for *everyone's* good in this."

After that I felt better. Still, sitting and waiting until it was time for Mom and Daddy to talk was scary. I looked around. These people were educated people, city people. Three more people oozed onto the end of our bench. We moved over. The youth group sang. They did a call-and-answer song that was really African. Usually I would have loved the complicated rhythm. Now I didn't even smile.

Finally Mom and Daddy went up. I could feel my heart beat in my ears. *Please just help them. Help Mom,* I prayed frantically over and over in my head.

Mom explained how Rick was born. Then she had to explain about the adoption, because in Kenya it's different. Illegitimate babies are always raised by grandparents and aunts and things. Daddy told how he and Mom had become Christians. Then they had decided to be missionaries. He said they hadn't hidden anything from the mission.

Then Daddy said, "We always prayed for Hazel's son. Now he is a man. He has looked for and found the mother who carried him in her body. We pray that he will also look for and find his heavenly Father. I'd like to ask all of our children to come forward so that you may see them."

My knees felt like rubber while we walked to the front. I looked at Rick. He had his chin up, but his face was red. At the front Daddy said, "These are our daughters, Sandy and Anika, whom you know. This is Rick Shaw, Hazel's son. He is studying in Oregon to be a veterinarian."

The people started to clap. Several called out, "Welcome! Welcome!"

After church they crowded around to greet us and welcome Rick. A lot of the people Mom had taught at Bible school were there. For me it was a blur of bright clothes and hands reaching to shake mine. I kept thinking about the baby elephant. Would he still be alive?

At Elanor Hales's place I burst out of the car. I was going to ask the first person I saw if our baby elephant was still alive. Instead, I stopped and stared. An older woman was standing there with her arm around an eland. It wasn't a baby eland, either. Eland are the biggest antelopes in Africa. She was talking to some people and patting the eland.

She looked over at us, then walked over. She was barefoot. The eland followed her.

"You must be the Scotts," she said. "I'm Elanor Hales."

Her voice was very English, clipped, and no-nonsense. She had kind eyes.

Daddy started introducing us. Halfway through I couldn't stand it anymore. I blurted, "Is he still alive? Is the baby elephant still alive? Can we see him?"

"Anika!" Mom said, but Elanor Hales laughed and said, "Yes, he is. He's still weak, but he has a good chance of surviving. We've named him Kioko. Daniel will show you around."

Daniel was an African man who explained things to us in English. There were two other small elephants and a partly grown rhino. All of them were having a mud bath out front.

Kioko was there with his mother-man. Each baby elephant had one. The mother-man's whole job was to take care of Kioko. He even slept near Kioko. Right then he was rubbing cool, muddy water behind Kioko's ear. Kioko leaned against him and touched him with his trunk. I wanted to go pet Kioko, but Daniel said no. He said Kioko needed to feel peacefully secure. It wouldn't be good for strangers to pet him yet.

Daniel explained that baby elephants die unless they feel safe and get lots and lots of touching and attention. The tiny ones used to die, even with lots of attention. Finally Mrs. Hales figured out how to make elephant milk formula. Now some stayed alive.

We had tea on the veranda of the low stone house. My finger traced the pattern on my elegant china teacup. I glanced over at Elanor Hales, wondering what her life was like.

"Hey," Rick said suddenly, "I'm doing exotic animal veterinary science. Is there any chance I could work with you summers?"

Mrs. Hales raised her eyebrows. "What do you mean by work?" she asked.

"Anything there is to do. I could learn immense amounts from you," he said.

"Yes," she said in a dry voice, "I'm sure you could. But what good would you be to me? I have workers already who know the animals."

Rick shrugged and raised his hands.

She laughed, "Write to me. I'll consider it."

Before we knew it, it was time to head for the airport. We had just been there for a few minutes when we heard the intercom boom, "Flight 172, KLM Nairobi to Amsterdam now boarding at Gate 3."

"That's my flight," Rick said. "Hey, I want to tell you before I go, I'm going to do some serious thinking about this whole Christianity thing. You all have made me see that the Creator God may be someone to take seriously."

Mom was frantically digging in her purse. She came up with the New Testament she always carries. She pushed it into Rick's hands. "I wanted to give you a Bible," she said, "but I was afraid to seem pushy. But now it sounds like you might not mind. The words in this book are more valuable than anything else I could possibly give you." She paused and smiled. "This Bible is beat up and full of underlining, but maybe it will remind you of our love."

"Thanks!" he said. "I'll read it."

The intercom announced his flight again. He hugged Sandy, then me. I only came up to his chest. "Thanks for the adventure, Sis," he said. "Get some more poachers for me."

He shook Daddy's hand and gave Mom a bear hug. Mom was crying when he walked through the security gate and out of sight. Even though I was going to miss Rick, I was excited about what he told us. Maybe he would get to be a Christian after all! I knew we would all keep praying for him and look forward to seeing him again.